NEW YORK REVIEW BOOKS
CLASSICS

PETER THE GREAT'S AFRICAN

ALEXANDER PUSHKIN (1799–1837) was born in Moscow and brought up mainly by tutors and governesses. One of his great-grandfathers, Abram Gannibal, was an African slave who became a favorite and the godson of Peter the Great. Like many aristocrats, Pushkin learned Russian mainly from household serfs.

As an adolescent, he attended the new elite lyceum at Tsarskoye Selo, outside St. Petersburg. In his early twenties he was exiled because of his political verse, first to the Caucasus, then to Odessa, then to his mother's estate in the north. Several of his friends took part in the failed 1825 Decembrist revolt, but Pushkin did not—possibly because his friends wished to protect him, possibly because they did not trust him to keep the plot secret. In 1826 Pushkin was allowed to return to St. Petersburg. During his last years he suffered many humiliations, including serious debts and worries about the fidelity of his young wife, Natalya Goncharova. In 1837 he was fatally wounded in a duel with Baron Georges d'Anthès, the Dutch ambassador's adopted son, who was said to be having an affair with Natalya.

Pushkin's position in Russian literature can best be compared with that of Goethe in Germany. Not only is he Russia's greatest poet; he is also the author of the first major works in a variety of genres. As well as his masterpieces—the verse novel *Eugene Onegin* and the narrative poem *The Bronze Horseman*—Pushkin wrote one of the first important Russian dramas, *Boris Godunov*; one of the finest of all Russian short stories, "The Queen of Spades"; and the first great Russian prose novel, *The Captain's Daughter* (published as an NYRB Classic). His prose style is clear and succinct; he wrote that "Precision and brevity are the most important qualities of prose. Prose demands thoughts and more thoughts—without thoughts, dazzling expressions serve no purpose."

ROBERT CHANDLER's translations from Russian include Alexander Pushkin's *The Captain's Daughter*; Nikolay Leskov's *Lady Macbeth of Mtsensk*; Vasily Grossman's *An Armenian Sketchbook*, *Everything Flows*, *Stalingrad*, *Life and Fate*, and *The Road* (all NYRB classics); and Hamid Ismailov's Central Asian novel, *The Railway*. His co-translations of Andrey Platonov have won prizes both in the UK and in the United States. He is the editor and main translator of *Russian Short Stories from Pushkin to Buida* and *Russian Magic Tales from Pushkin to Platonov*. Together with Boris Dralyuk and Irina Mashinski he co-edited *The Penguin Book of Russian Poetry*. He also translated selections of Sappho and Apollinaire. As well as running regular translation workshops in London and teaching at an annual literary translation summer school, he works as a mentor at the British Centre for Literary Translation.

ELIZABETH CHANDLER is a co-translator, with her husband, of Pushkin's *The Captain's Daughter*; of Vasily Grossman's *Stalingrad*, *Everything Flows*, *An Armenian Sketchbook*, and *The Road*; and of several works by Andrey Platonov.

BORIS DRALYUK is the editor in chief of the *Los Angeles Review of Books*; translator of Isaac Babel, Maxim Osipov, Mikhail Zoshchenko, and others; and author of *My Hollywood and Other Poems*.

PETER THE GREAT'S AFRICAN

Experiments in Prose

ALEXANDER PUSHKIN

Translated from the Russian by
ROBERT *and* **ELIZABETH CHANDLER**
and **BORIS DRALYUK**

NEW YORK REVIEW BOOKS

New York

THIS IS A NEW YORK REVIEW BOOK
PUBLISHED BY THE NEW YORK REVIEW OF BOOKS
435 Hudson Street, New York, NY 10014
www.nyrb.com

 transcript

The publication was effected in part under the auspices of the Mikhail Prokhorov Foundation TRANSCRIPT Programme to Support Translations of Russian Literature

Library of Congress Cataloging-in-Publication Data
Names: Pushkin, Aleksandr Sergeevich, 1799–1837, author. | Chandler, Robert, 1953– translator. | Chandler, Elizabeth, 1947– translator. | Dralyuk, Boris, translator. | Pushkin, Aleksandr Sergeevich, 1799–1837. Arap Petra Velikogo. English | Pushkin, Aleksandr Sergeevich, 1799–1837. Istorii͡a sela Gori͡ukhina. English | Pushkin, Aleksandr Sergeevich, 1799–1837. Dubrovskiĭ. English | Pushkin, Aleksandr Sergeevich, 1799–1837. Egipetskie nochi. English
Title: Peter the Great's African : experiments in prose / by Alexander Pushkin; translated by Robert Chandler & Elizabeth Chandler and Boris Dralyuk.
Description: New York: New York Review Books, [2022] | Series: New York Review Books classics
Identifiers: LCCN 2021012396 (print) | LCCN 2021012397 (ebook) | ISBN 9781681375991 (paperback) | ISBN 9781681376004 (ebook)
Subjects: LCSH: Pushkin, Aleksandr Sergeevich, 1799–1837—Translations into English. | LCGFT: Novels.
Classification: LCC PG3347.A2 C47 2021 (print) | LCC PG3347.A2 (ebook) | DDC 891.73/3—dc23
LC record available at https://lccn.loc.gov/2021012396
LC ebook record available at https://lccn.loc.gov/2021012397

ISBN 978-1-68137-599-1
Available as an electronic book; ISBN ISBN 978-1-68137-600-4

Printed in the United States of America on acid-free paper.
10 9 8 7 6 5 4 3 2 1

CONTENTS

PREFACE

BORN IN Moscow, Alexander Sergeyevich Pushkin was brought up
mainly by tutors and governesses. One of his great-grandfathers,
Abram Gannibal (ca. 1696–1781), was an African slave who became
a favorite and godson of Peter the Great's. Like many aristocratic
children of his time, Pushkin learned Russian from household serfs;
until the Napoleonic Wars, the aristocracy still spoke French rather
than Russian.

In his early twenties, because of his political poems, Pushkin was
exiled—first to the south of Russia, then to Mikhailovskoye, his
mother's family's estate in the north. Several of his friends took part
in the Decembrist Revolt of 1825, but Pushkin did not—perhaps
simply because his friends considered him dangerously indiscreet. In
1826 Pushkin returned to St. Petersburg, with Tsar Nicholas I, promising him that he would no longer need to submit his work to the
censorship; instead, he himself would be his censor. During his last
years Pushkin suffered many humiliations, including serious debts
and worries about the fidelity of his young wife, Natalya Goncharova.
He was fatally wounded in a duel with Baron Georges d'Anthès, the
Dutch ambassador's adopted son, who was rumored to be having an
affair with Natalya.

Pushkin's importance in Russian literature is still greater than
that of Shakespeare and Dante in their respective national literatures.
He perhaps has more in common with Goethe. Not only is he Russia's
greatest poet, but he is also the author of foundational works in many
different genres. As well as his masterpieces—the verse novel *Eugene
Onegin* and the narrative poem *The Bronze Horseman*—Pushkin

wrote one of the first important Russian dramas, *Boris Godunov*; the first major Russian historical novel, *The Captain's Daughter*; and one of the greatest of all Russian short stories, "The Queen of Spades."

Russians of all political persuasions and artistic schools have always seen Pushkin as the embodiment of something uniquely precious. Few people have written better about him than the dissident writer and scholar Andrey Sinyavsky. In *Strolls with Pushkin* (a high-spirited book composed in the late 1960s, in a labor camp, and sent out in installments in letters to his wife), he declares,

> Pushkin is the golden mean of Russian literature. Having kicked Russian literature headlong into the future, he [...] now plays in it the role of an eternally flowering past to which it returns in order to become younger. The moment a new talent appears, there we see Pushkin with his prompts and crib notes—and generations to come, decades from now, will again find Pushkin standing behind them. If we take ourselves back in thought to far-off times, to the sources of our native tongue, there too we will find Pushkin—further back still, earlier still, on the eve of the first chronicles and songs. An archaic smile plays on his lips.[1]

Pushkin is nearly always referred to as a poet, though he wrote an almost equal quantity of prose. Poetry came more easily to him; he wrote poetry prolifically and seemed able to master almost any genre. Prose, on the other hand, was something he had to work at more consciously. He very much wanted to write prose fiction—in part out of a desire to write more barely and simply, in part because the reading public was losing interest in poetry and he needed to earn a living—but during the last ten years of his life he repeatedly found himself unable to complete stories and novels that had begun promisingly. In 1833, he said to the Russian scholar and lexicographer, Vladimir Dal', "You wouldn't believe how much I long to write a novel, yet I cannot. I have begun three of them. I start off perfectly well, but then I run out of patience and cannot manage."[2]

The Captain's Daughter, Pushkin's one finished novel, is a masterpiece—perhaps the subtlest and most delicately constructed of all nineteenth-century Russian novels. Several of the unfinished stories and novels, however, are hardly less remarkable. They are of interest both in their own right and for the insight they allow us into Pushkin's creative laboratory.

—ROBERT CHANDLER

PETER THE GREAT'S AFRICAN

PETER THE GREAT'S AFRICAN

Through Peter's iron will
Russia has been transformed.

—Nikolay Yazykov[1]

I

I am in Paris:
I've begun to live, not just to breathe.
            —IVAN DMITRIEV, "A Traveller's Diary"[2]

PETER the Great sent a number of young men to foreign lands to acquire knowledge necessary to a Russia he had transformed; among them was his godson, an African named Ibrahim. The young man studied at the École Militaire in Paris, graduated with the rank of artillery captain, distinguished himself in the war against Spain,[3] and then, after being seriously wounded, returned to Paris. Absorbed though the tsar was in his vast undertakings, he often inquired after his young favorite and always received glowing reports of his progress and conduct. This greatly pleased Peter and he repeatedly summoned his godson home, but Ibrahim was in no hurry. He excused himself on various pretexts—his wound, his desire to complete his studies, a lack of funds—and Peter always relented. He urged Ibrahim to take care of his health, praised his thirst for knowledge, and, though always extremely frugal in regard to his own expenses, gave generously from his Treasury, accompanying the gold coins with fatherly words of caution and counsel.

As all the historical records testify, nothing could compare with the willful frivolity, madness, and luxury of the French at that time. The final years of the reign of Louis XIV, which had been marked by strict piety at court, by dignity and solemnity, had left not a trace behind. The Duke of Orléans,[4] in whom innumerable brilliant qualities commingled with vices of every sort, was woefully devoid of hypocrisy. The orgies at the Palais-Royal were an open secret in Paris; their example proved contagious. Just then John Law came to town;[5] avarice joined with a thirst for enjoyment and dissipation; estates and fortunes were frittered away; morality perished; the French laughed and speculated while the state disintegrated to the playful refrains of satirical vaudevilles.

Meanwhile, society presented a most entertaining spectacle. Sophistication and the need for amusement brought together all the estates. Wealth, affability, fame, talent, mere eccentricity—anything that might pique curiosity or promise pleasure was welcomed with equal enthusiasm. Literature, scholarship, and philosophy abandoned their quiet libraries and made their appearance in high society, both complying with fashion and informing its opinions. Women reigned, but they no longer demanded adoration. Superficial gallantry took the place of profound respect. The escapades of the Duke of Richelieu, that Alcibiades of a latter-day Athens, have been well documented and provide a glimpse of the era's mores:[6]

> But now behold those happy days advance,
> When pleasing Folly reigns supreme in France;
> Rattling her bells throughout the merry land,
> She scatters blessings with a liberal hand;
> Each whim indulging, each eccentric notion,
> And nought was strange in France, except devotion.[7]

The arrival of Ibrahim—his appearance, his education, his native intelligence—set Paris abuzz. All the ladies wished to receive *le Nègre du czar* and vied with one another to have him attend their salons; the regent invited him to more than one of his merry soirées; he attended suppers enlivened by the young Voltaire and the elderly Chaulieu, and by the conversation of Montesquieu and Fontenelle;[8] he missed not a single ball, not a single debut, not a single festivity of any kind, and he threw himself into the whirl of social life with all the ardor of his age and race. But what terrified Ibrahim was not merely the thought of exchanging this dissipation, these brilliant amusements, for the severe simplicity of the Petersburg court. The young African was bound to Paris by stronger ties. He was in love.

The Countess D., though no longer in the first bloom of her youth, was still famed for her beauty. At the age of seventeen, on leaving her convent school, she had been given in marriage to a man she had not yet come to love; and her husband had never tried to set this right. Gossip ascribed several lovers to her, but she was treated with indulgence and allowed to retain her good name, for there was never anything laughable or embarrassing about her liaisons. Her home was among the most fashionable, frequented by the finest Parisian society. Ibrahim was introduced to her by the young Merville, who was thought to be the most recent of her lovers and who had done all he could to confirm that reputation.

The countess received Ibrahim courteously, but without any excessive ado; he found this flattering. People usually looked upon the young Black man as some kind of wonder, clustering around him and showering him with greetings and questions. This general curiosity—veiled though it was by an air of goodwill—wounded his self-esteem. The sweet attention of the opposite sex, almost the only goal of all our strivings, not only failed to gladden his heart but even filled it with bitterness and indignation. He felt that women saw him as some kind of rare beast, a peculiar, alien creature accidentally transported to a world with which it had nothing in common. Indeed, he envied people who went entirely unnoticed, thinking them fortunate in their dullness.

The thought that nature had not intended him for reciprocated passion freed him from conceit and the pretensions of pride, lending a rare charm to his manner with women. His conversation was simple and dignified. All this appealed to the Countess D., who was tired of the endless jests and subtle insinuations of French wit. Ibrahim was a frequent guest at her home. Little by little, she grew accustomed to the young man's looks, and even began to take pleasure in seeing his curly black head amid the sea of powdered wigs in her drawing room. (Ibrahim had been wounded in the head and wore a bandage instead of a wig.) He was twenty-seven years old, tall and well built, and more than one beautiful woman had glanced at him with a look more flattering than mere curiosity, but Ibrahim, in his prejudice, either did not notice these glances or saw in them only coquetry. Yet when his eyes met those of the countess, his mistrust vanished. Her gaze was so sweetly good-natured, her manner towards him so straightforward, so unaffected that it was impossible to suspect her of even the slightest coquetry or mockery.

The possibility of love had not crossed his mind, but he could no longer go a day without seeing the countess. He sought for every opportunity to meet her, yet every meeting seemed to him an unexpected favor from heaven. The countess divined his feelings before he did. Whatever anybody may say, love without hope or demands is more certain to touch a woman's heart than all the artifices of seduction. When they were together, the countess followed Ibrahim's every movement and listened closely to his every word; when they were apart, she grew pensive and relapsed into her usual abstraction... Merville was the first to notice this mutual affection. He congratulated Ibrahim. Nothing inflames love like an encouraging remark from an observer. Love is blind and, unsure of its footing, hastily clutches at every support. Merville's words awaked Ibrahim. He had never so much as imagined the possibility of possessing the woman he loved. All at once, the light of hope illumined his soul; he fell head over heels. Frightened by the frenzy of his passion, the countess tried in vain to fend it off with friendly admonitions and prudent advice, but she herself was weakening. Reckless favors were granted in quick succession. And at last, overcome and swept away by the force of a passion she herself had inspired, the countess surrendered to the enraptured Ibrahim.

Nothing escapes the sharp eyes of society. The news of the countess's latest liaison soon became common knowledge. A few ladies were astonished at her choice, while many others found it entirely natural. Some laughed; others thought her guilty of unpardonable indiscretion. In the first transports of their passion, Ibrahim and the countess were oblivious to everything, but then they began to notice the barbed remarks of certain women and the double entendres uttered by men. Ibrahim's cool and dignified demeanor had hitherto shielded him from such gibes, but now he found them hard to endure and did not know how to avert them. The countess, accustomed as she was to the respect of society, did not like being the target of gossip and ridicule. Now she would tearfully complain to Ibrahim, now bitterly reproach him, now beg him not to intervene on her behalf, lest some vain squabble bring about her total downfall.

Her position was further complicated by a new circumstance: the consequence of careless love. Counsel, suggestions, words of consolation—all were exhausted, all rejected. The countess could see only inevitable ruin and she awaited it in despair.

As soon as her predicament became apparent, rumors began to circulate with still greater intensity. Sensitive ladies let out gasps of horror, while men laid bets on whether the child would be white or black. There was no end to epigrams upon her husband—the only person in Paris who knew and suspected nothing.

The fateful moment drew nearer. The countess was distraught. Ibrahim visited her daily. He saw her growing weaker, both spiritually and physically. Her tears, her terror increased with every moment. Finally, she felt the first pangs of labor. Measures were quickly taken. They managed to get the count out of the way. The doctor arrived. Two days earlier, some indigent woman had been persuaded to give away her newborn son; a confidant was now sent to fetch this child. Ibrahim waited in a study adjoining the room where the unfortunate countess was lying. Hardly daring to breathe, he listened to her stifled moans, the nurse's whispers, and the doctor's commands. She suffered for a long time. Her every moan tore at his soul, while every interval of silence filled him with dread ... Suddenly he heard the weak cry of a child. Unable to restrain his joy, he rushed into the countess's room; a black baby lay on the bed by her feet. Ibrahim went up closer. His heart was pounding. His hand trembling, he made the sign of the cross over his son. The countess gave a faint smile and reached out weakly towards him—but the doctor, fearing that such excitement might harm the patient, pulled Ibrahim away from her bed. The newborn was placed in a covered basket and taken out by way of a secret staircase. The other child was brought in and its cradle placed in the bedroom. Somewhat calmer now, Ibrahim left the house. Now they awaited the count. He came home late, learned of his wife's successful delivery, and was very pleased. And so the public, which had anticipated drama and scandal, was forced to make do with mere hearsay.

Everything returned to normal. But Ibrahim felt that his fate was bound to change; sooner or later, word of the illicit union would reach Count D. Come what may, the countess's ruin would then be inevitable. Ibrahim loved passionately and was beloved with equal passion—but the countess was willful and flighty. This was not her first affair. Hatred and revulsion might take the place of the most tender feelings. Ibrahim foresaw the moment her heart would cool towards him; he had never known jealousy, but he now felt an awful presentiment of it. He imagined that the sorrows of parting would be less agonizing, and so he began to think about breaking off this ill-starred liaison, leaving Paris, and returning to Russia, where both Peter and his own uncertain sense of duty had long been calling him.

2

...No more
Does beauty tempt me as it did,
Less often am I rapt with joy,
My mind is not so free to roam,
I am less easy with my fate:
The thirst for honors tears my soul,
I hear the urgent call of fame.

—GAVRILA DERZHAVIN[9]

DAYS AND months went by, but Ibrahim, who was still in love, could not bring himself to leave the woman he had seduced. The countess grew fonder of him hour by hour. Their son was being brought up far from the capital. The gossip was gradually dying down, and the lovers were now enjoying more tranquility, recalling the storms of their past in silence while trying not to think about the future.

One day Ibrahim attended a reception given by the Duke of Orléans. As the duke passed by him, he stopped and handed him a letter, telling Ibrahim to read it at his leisure. The letter was from Peter I. Having guessed at the true cause of his foster son's long absence, the sovereign had written to the duke to explain that he had no intention of imposing his will on the young man. Ibrahim was free to decide whether or not to return to Russia; whatever his decision, Peter would never withdraw his support. This letter touched Ibrahim to the very depths of his soul. From that moment, his fate was decided. The next day he told the duke that he intended to set off soon for Russia.

"Think about what you are doing," said the duke. "Russia is not your native country. I doubt you will ever set eyes on your sultry homeland again, but your long sojourn in France has spoiled you for both the climate and the way of life of half-barbarous Russia. You were not born a subject of Peter's. Take my advice: make the most of his gracious forbearance. Stay in France, a country for which you have already shed your blood. You can be sure that here too your merits and talents will not go unrewarded." Ibrahim offered the duke his sincerest thanks, but he remained firm. "A pity," the duke replied. "Nonetheless, you are right." He promised Ibrahim an honorable discharge and reported all this to the tsar.

Soon Ibrahim was ready for the journey. He spent the evening before his departure in the usual manner, at the home of Countess D. She knew nothing of his plans; Ibrahim had not the heart to tell her. The countess was calm and cheerful. Several times she called him to her side and poked gentle fun at his pensiveness. After supper, the other guests left. The countess remained in the drawing room with her husband and Ibrahim. Poor Ibrahim would have given anything in the world to be left alone with her—but Count D. seemed so comfortably settled beside the fire that there seemed no hope of dislodging him. The three of them sat in silence. At last, the countess spoke: "*Bonne nuit.*" Ibrahim's heart sank and he suddenly felt the full anguish of imminent parting. He stood stock-still. "*Bonne nuit, messieurs,*" repeated the countess. Ibrahim still did not move...At last, with difficulty—his vision dim, his head reeling—he made his way out of the room. When he got back to his home, he wrote, in an almost unconscious state, the following letter:

I am going away, dear Leonora. I am leaving you forever. I write this because I lack the courage to explain myself in any other way.

My happiness was doomed from the start; both fate and nature were against it. Your love was sure to fade, the enchantment sure to vanish. This thought always haunted me—even at moments when I appeared to forget everything, when I lay at your feet, intoxicated by your passionate self-sacrifice, your boundless tenderness...Light-headed society ruthlessly punishes in practice what it permits in theory: sooner or later, its cold mockery would have defeated you, taming your fiery heart, and you would have grown ashamed of your passion...What would have become of me then? No! I would rather die—I would rather leave you before that terrible moment...

Nothing is dearer to me than your peace of mind: with the eyes of the world upon us, you were unable to enjoy it. Remember all that you have endured—the wounds to your pride, the torments of fear...Remember the birth of our son. Ask yourself: is it right for me to expose you to such turmoil and danger? Why should we strive to unite the fate of so tender and beautiful a being as yourself with the terrible fate of a Negro—a pitiful creature scarcely worthy of being called human?

Farewell, Leonora, my dear, my only friend. Leaving you, I leave the first and last joys of my life. I have no fatherland, no kin. I depart for sad Russia, where I shall have no joy but my perfect solitude. Exacting work, to which I shall now devote myself, will not silence the tormenting recollections of our days of rapture and bliss, but it will at least distract me from them... Farewell, Leonora—I tear myself from this letter as if tearing myself from your arms. Farewell, be happy—and, from time to time, give a thought to your poor Negro, your faithful Ibrahim.

That same night he departed for Russia.

The journey did not prove as grim as he had expected. Ibrahim's imagination prevailed over reality. As he traveled farther and farther from Paris, all that he had abandoned forever grew more and more vivid to him, more and more real.

Before he knew it, he had reached the Russian border. Autumn was already setting in, but the coachmen, in spite of the bad roads, drove him as fast as the wind; and so, on the morning of the seventeenth day of his journey, he arrived in Krasnoye Selo,[10] through which the high road used to pass.

They were eighteen miles from Petersburg. While the horses were being changed, Ibrahim went into the post station. A tall man in a green kaftan was sitting in the corner with his elbows on the table and a clay pipe in his mouth, reading the Hamburg newspapers.[11] Hearing someone enter, he looked up. "Ibrahim? My dear boy!" he shouted, rising from the bench. "Greetings, godson!" Recognizing Peter, Ibrahim was overcome with joy. He wanted to rush towards him but, out of respect, restrained himself. The sovereign approached him, embraced him, and kissed him on the head. "I was told you were on your way," he said, "so I decided to meet you. I've been waiting since yesterday." Ibrahim could not find words to express his gratitude. "Have your carriage follow ours," the sovereign continued. "You must come in mine."

Peter's carriage was brought up; he and Ibrahim took their seats and the horses set off at a gallop. An hour and a half later, they were in Petersburg. Ibrahim was intrigued to see the newborn capital being conjured from the swamp by autocracy. Wherever he looked, exposed dams, wooden bridges, and canals without embankments testified to the recent triumph of human will over the resistance of nature. The houses all looked as if built in haste. There was nothing magnificent apart from the Neva, which had not yet been adorned with its granite frame but was already covered with both military and merchant vessels. The sovereign's carriage stopped at the palace in the Tsaritsyn Garden. There, on the portico, Peter was met by a beautiful woman of about thirty-five, who was dressed after the latest Parisian fashions.[12] Peter kissed her on the lips and, taking Ibrahim by the hand, said, "Catherine, my dear—do you recognize my godson? I ask you to love and favor him as you did long ago." Catherine fixed her black, penetrating eyes on Ibrahim and graciously offered her hand. Two young beauties—tall, slim, and fresh as roses—were standing behind her. They went respectfully up to Peter. "Liza," the sovereign said to one of them, "do you remember the little African who used to steal my apples in Oranienbaum and give them to you? Well, let me introduce him to you." The grand duchess[13] laughed and blushed. They went through to the dining room. The table was already laid, and Peter invited Ibrahim to eat with him and his family. During the meal Peter talked to the young man about a variety of topics, asking him about the war against Spain, French internal affairs, and the Duke of Orléans—a man he was fond of, despite his evident flaws. Ibrahim was endowed with a precise, observant mind, and his answers greatly pleased Peter. Peter recalled certain episodes from Ibrahim's childhood, relating them in such a cheerful, kindhearted manner that no one would have suspected this courteous and welcoming host of being the hero of Poltava,[14] the mighty, fearsome transformer of Russia.

When they had finished eating, Peter retired to rest, in the Russian way, while Ibrahim stayed behind with the empress and the grand duchesses. He did his best to satisfy their curiosity, describing in detail the way of life, the festivities, and the capricious fashions he had witnessed in Paris. In the meantime, they were joined by several of the men closest to the sovereign. Ibrahim recognized Prince Yakov Dolgoruky, Peter's stern adviser; the magisterial Prince Menshikov, who, on seeing an African talking to Catherine, gave him a haughty sidelong glance; the learned Bruce, who enjoyed the reputation of a Russian Faust; young Raguzinsky, Ibrahim's childhood friend; and others who had come to the sovereign with reports and who were awaiting his orders.[15]

About two hours later, Peter reappeared. "Let's see if you can still manage your old duties," he said to Ibrahim. "Take a slate and come with me." Peter closed the door of his carpenter's workshop and turned to affairs of state. He worked first with Bruce, then with Prince Dolgoruky, then with De Vière, the general chief of police.[16] He dictated several decrees and edicts to Ibrahim, who could not but marvel at the quickness and firmness of Peter's mind, at the force and flexibility of his attention, and at the range of his concerns and activities. Finally, Peter drew a notebook from his pocket so as to assure himself that he had indeed completed all the day's tasks. As he was leaving the workshop, he turned to Ibrahim and said, "It's late. You must be tired. Spend the night here, like in the old days. I'll come and wake you tomorrow."

Left alone, Ibrahim struggled to collect his thoughts. He was back in Petersburg, in the company of that great man in whose home, not yet aware of his true worth, he had spent his childhood. In his heart he confessed, almost remorsefully, that, for the first time since their parting, there had been moments when he was not thinking about the Countess D. He saw that the new life awaiting him—a life of constant activity—might revive his soul, weakened by passion, idleness, and a secret despair. The prospect of serving beside a great man, of joining him in shaping the destiny of a great people, aroused in him, for the first time, the noble feeling of ambition. It was with these thoughts that he lay down in the camp bed prepared for him—but soon his dreams took him away to distant Paris, into the arms of his dear countess.

3

Like clouds high in the sky,
Our thoughts shift their soft shapes within us:
Tomorrow we will hate what we now love.
—WILHELM KÜCHELBECKER[17]

THE NEXT morning Peter woke Ibrahim, as promised, and congratulated him on being appointed captain-lieutenant of the Preobrazhensky Regiment's Artillery Company, of which he himself was the captain. Peter's courtiers gathered around Ibrahim, each trying in his own way to flatter the new favorite. The haughty Prince Menshikov gave him a cordial handshake; Sheremetev asked about various people he knew in Paris; and Golovin invited Ibrahim to dinner.[18] Others followed this last example, and soon Ibrahim had received at least a month's worth of invitations.

Ibrahim's days all took the same shape but were filled with activity; there was no time to feel bored. With each day he felt more devoted to the sovereign, better able to appreciate his lofty mind. To follow the thoughts of a great man is the most absorbing of activities. Ibrahim saw Peter in the Senate, disputing with Buturlin[19] and Dolgoruky and examining important legislative matters; in the Admiralty Collegium, affirming Russia's maritime might; at leisure, poring over translations of foreign thinkers in the company of Feofan, Kopievich, and Gavril Buzhinsky;[20] or making the rounds of warehouses, workshops, and libraries. To Ibrahim, all of Russia seemed like a vast factory where only machines were in motion, where every worker was carrying out his work according to a well-established routine. He considered himself to be just such a worker, duty bound to operate his lathe—and he tried to mourn the delights of life in Paris as little as possible. Alas, another tender recollection proved harder to dispel: he often thought of Countess D., imagining her righteous indignation, her tears, her despair... And then, at times, he was seized by a dreadful presentiment: the distractions of the beau monde, a new liaison, another man enjoying her favors—and he would shudder, his African blood boiling with jealousy, hot tears ready to stream down his black cheeks.

One morning as he sat in his study, surrounded by documents, he heard a loud greeting in French. He quickly turned around—and young Korsakov, whom he had last seen in the whirl of Parisian society, embraced him with exclamations of joy.[21] "I've just arrived," said Korsakov, "and I've hurried straight over. All our Parisian friends send their greetings and say how much they regret your absence. Countess D. commanded me to summon you back without fail. Here, she's written you a letter." Ibrahim snatched it, his heart trembling, and stared at the familiar handwriting of the address, not daring to believe his eyes. "How glad I am," Korsakov went on, "that you have not yet died of boredom in this barbarous Petersburg! What do people do here? How do they pass the time? Who's your tailor? Is there even an opera house?" Ibrahim, his mind elsewhere, replied that the sovereign was probably working at the shipyard. "I can see," Korsakov said with a laugh, "that you don't have time for me now. Your mind's on other things. We'll talk later. I'll go and present myself to the sovereign." And he spun round on one heel and dashed out of the room.

The moment he was alone, Ibrahim unsealed the letter. With great tenderness, the countess was reproaching him for his mistrust and lack of openness. "You say," she wrote, "that nothing is dearer to you than my peace of mind. Oh, Ibrahim! Were that true, would you have chosen to make me suffer as I have suffered since your sudden departure? You feared that I would detain you, but I assure you that, no matter how much I love you, I would have sacrificed my love for your well-being and for what you consider to be your duty." The countess ended her letter with passionate assurances of love, imploring Ibrahim, if there was truly no hope of their meeting again, to write to her at least occasionally.

Ibrahim read the letter no fewer than twenty times, delightedly kissing its precious lines. He was anxious to hear more about the countess and was about to leave for the Admiralty, where he hoped to find Korsakov, when the door to his study opened and Korsakov reappeared. He had already presented himself to the sovereign and, as always, seemed rather pleased with himself.

"*Entre nous*," he said to Ibrahim, "the sovereign is a mighty odd man. Just imagine—I found him wearing some sort of sackcloth blouse, high up on the mast of a new ship. Well, I had no choice but to clamber up there with my dispatches. There I was, perched on a rope ladder, without enough space to make a proper bow. Let me tell you, I was at a loss—as never before in all my life. However, after the sovereign read my papers, he looked me over from head to foot and was, I think, rather impressed by the tasteful elegance of my attire. At any rate, he smiled and invited me to this evening's assembly.[22] But I am a perfect foreigner in Petersburg! After six years in France, I've completely forgotten the local customs. Please be my mentor—pick me up this evening and introduce me." Ibrahim readily agreed and quickly turned the conversation to matters of more personal interest. "Well, how is the Countess D.?" "The countess? Well, at first, she was very much grieved by your departure. But you know how these things go—she got over it little by little and then she took a new lover. Guess who? That gangly Marquis of R. Now put those blackamoor eyes back in their sockets! Is it really so surprising? Don't you know that protracted grief is alien to human nature, especially to a woman's? Think about it. But now, after my journey, I need a rest. And don't forget to come and pick me up."

What feelings welled up in Ibrahim's heart? Jealousy? Rage? Despair? No—only profound, stifling gloom. He kept repeating to himself, "I knew it. It was bound to happen." Then he opened the countess's letter once more, reread it, hung his head, and wept bitterly. He wept for a long time, and the tears eased his heart. Looking at his watch, he saw that it was time to leave. He would have been only too glad to miss the assembly, but it was his official duty to attend; the sovereign required the presence of his confidants. And so Ibrahim dressed and went to fetch Korsakov.

Korsakov was sitting in his dressing room, reading a French book. "So early?" he said on seeing Ibrahim. "For heaven's sake!" Ibrahim replied. "It's already half past five. We're going to be late. Get dressed and let's go!" Korsakov began to bustle about, ringing for his servants with all his might. They came running; he hurriedly began to dress. His French valet handed him shoes with red heels, trousers of blue velvet, and a pink kaftan embroidered with spangles. His wig was quickly powdered in the anteroom, brought in, and slipped onto his closely cropped head. He asked for his sword and gloves, took ten turns in front of the mirror, and announced to Ibrahim that he was ready. The footmen helped the two men into their bearskin coats and they set off for the Winter Palace.

Korsakov bombarded Ibrahim with questions: Who was the greatest beauty in Petersburg? Who was the finest dancer? What dance was currently in vogue? Ibrahim had no choice but to satisfy his friend's curiosity—and before long they reached the palace. There were vehicles everywhere—long sleighs, old-fashioned carriages, and gilded coaches. The portico was crowded with the entourage considered indispensable by the boyars of those days.[23] There were liveried, bewhiskered coachmen, hussars and pages, mace-wielding servants adorned with gold braid and feathers, and clumsy footmen weighed down by their masters' furs and muffs. A murmur rose from the crowd as Ibrahim approached: "The African, the African, the tsar's African!" Ibrahim quickly led Korsakov through the motley horde. A palace footman flung the doors open and they went through to the hall. Korsakov was struck dumb.

In a large room lit by tallow candles—burning wanly amid the clouds of tobacco smoke—grandees with blue sashes across their chests,[24] ambassadors, foreign merchants, Guards officers in their green uniforms, and shipmasters in short jackets and striped trousers moved back and forth to the uninterrupted strains of a wind orchestra.[25] The ladies were seated along the walls. The younger ones were resplendent, their luxurious attire shining with gold and silver. Their narrow waists rose like little stems from their splendid farthingales; diamonds glittered in their ears, on their long curls, and around their necks. They looked about gaily, waiting to be asked for the first dance. The more elderly ladies, on the other hand, had made artful attempts to combine the new manner of dress with the now-outlawed styles of the past; their bonnets looked rather like Tsaritsa Natalya Kirilovna's sable cap,[26] while their gowns and mantles were somehow reminiscent of *sarafans* and quilted "soul-warmers." They appeared to be attending these newfangled functions with more perplexity than pleasure, and they looked askance at the Dutch skippers' wives and daughters, evidently finding it hard to imagine how these women in red blouses and dimity skirts could carry on laughing, chatting, and knitting their stockings as if they were in their own homes.

Korsakov could make no sense of anything. Seeing him and Ibrahim, a servant came over, carrying a tray with bottles of beer and some glasses. "*Que diable est-ce que tout cela?*" Korsakov whispered to Ibrahim. Ibrahim could not help but smile. The empress and the grand duchesses, radiantly beautiful and exquisitely attired, were walking between the rows of guests, conversing affably with them.

Wanting to present himself to the sovereign, who was in another room, Korsakov fought his way through the constantly moving crowd. When he reached the door, he saw a large number of foreigners, solemnly smoking their clay pipes and draining clay mugs. On the tables were bottles of beer and wine, leather pouches full of tobacco, glasses of punch, and chessboards. At one of these tables, Peter and a broad-shouldered English skipper were playing checkers, diligently saluting each other with sudden blasts of tobacco smoke. The sovereign was so surprised by an unexpected move of his opponent's that he failed to notice Korsakov, who was hovering around the table. Then a stout gentleman with a large bouquet pinned to his chest burst into the room, boomed out that the dance had begun, then withdrew. A large number of people, Korsakov among them, followed him out.

Korsakov was astounded by the spectacle before him. Facing each other, the entire length of the hall, stood two rows of people—a row of ladies and a row of gentlemen. To the sound of the most mournful music, the gentlemen bowed low and the ladies curtseyed even lower—first to the front, then to the right, then to the left, to the front again, and to the right, and so on. Korsakov bit his lip, staring wide-eyed at this intricate pastime. The bows and curtseys continued for nearly half an hour. At last the stout gentleman with the bouquet declared that the ceremonies were now over and commanded the musicians to strike up a minuet. Korsakov was overjoyed: this was his moment to shine. Among the younger guests there was one he had singled out. She looked about sixteen years old and was dressed sumptuously but with taste. She was sitting next to an elderly man who looked rather stern and imposing. Korsakov flew to the young beauty and asked her to honor him with a dance. She gazed at him in confusion, apparently not knowing how to respond, while the man beside her frowned more sternly than ever. Korsakov was still awaiting her decision when the gentleman with the bouquet came over to him, led him to the center of the hall, and solemnly pronounced, "Sir, you have committed a grave impropriety—first, by going up to the young lady without making the requisite three bows, and second, by taking it upon yourself to choose her, whereas, in the minuet, the right to choose a partner belongs to the lady. For this you are to be punished severely—namely, you are to drain the Goblet of the Great Eagle."

Korsakov's bewilderment had been growing from hour to hour. Other guests instantly surrounded him, boisterously demanding the immediate execution of the sentence. Hearing shouts and laughter, Peter emerged from the adjoining room; he very much liked to be present in person at such punishments. The crowd parted and Peter entered the circle where the marshal of the assembly, holding an enormous goblet of malmsey, was standing before the criminal. The marshal was trying, in vain, to persuade the offender to submit to the law of his own free will. "Aha!" said Peter. "You're in for it now, Brother. Be so good, monsieur, as to wipe that frown off your face and drink up." What could Korsakov do? The poor fop took the goblet, downed the malmsey in one, and handed it back to the marshal. "See here, Korsakov," Peter continued. "Those breeches of yours are made of velvet. Even I wouldn't allow myself such an extravagance, and I'm a great deal richer than you. Take care now, I don't want to have to speak to you again."

After this rebuke, Korsakov tried to make his way out of the circle—but he staggered and nearly fell, to the indescribable pleasure of the sovereign and the whole merry crowd. Far from spoiling the harmony of the main part of the evening's entertainment, this little episode served only to enliven it. The gentlemen went back to bowing and shuffling, while the ladies curtseyed and tapped their heels with great zeal, no longer troubling to keep time with the music. Korsakov was in no state to join in the general revelry. The young beauty came up to Ibrahim—evidently at a word from her father; looking down at the floor with her pale-blue eyes, she demurely extended her hand. Ibrahim danced the minuet with her, then led her back to her seat and went in search of Korsakov. He escorted his friend out of the hall, sat him in a carriage, and took him back home. During the first part of the journey, Korsakov kept muttering, "Damned assembly... Damned golden eagle goblet..." But soon he fell into a deep sleep. He had no sense at all of how he got home, how he was undressed, and how he was put to bed. The next day he awoke with a headache and only vague recollections of the shuffling and curtseying, the tobacco smoke, the gentleman with the bouquet, and the Goblet of the Great Eagle.[27]

4

Our fathers gave each meal its due.
They took their time to drink and dine.
With dignity, they passed around
The mugs of beer and cups of wine.

— *Ruslan and Ludmila*[28]

NOW I MUST introduce the gentle reader to Gavrila Afanasevich Rzhevsky. A scion of an ancient boyar family, he loved falconry, was noted for his hospitality, and owned a vast estate, manned by workers of every kind. In a word, he was a Russian nobleman through and through. He could not stand any hint of Germanism, as he liked to put it, and he did his best to preserve the old ways he held so dear.

His daughter was seventeen. After losing her mother while still a child, she had been raised in the traditional manner—that is, amid nurses, nannies, maids, and other girls of her own age. She had been taught to embroider with gold but not to read or write. And yet, despite his loathing for all things foreign, her father was unable to oppose her desire to learn German dances from the captive Swedish officer who lived in their home. This worthy dancing-master was about fifty years old. His right leg had been shot through at the battle of Narva[29] and was therefore ill suited to minuets and courantes; his left leg, however, could execute the most difficult *pas* with astonishing ease. Natalya Gavrilovna was a credit to that leg's endeavors. She was thought to be the finest dancer at the assemblies, which partly accounts for the degree of attention given to Korsakov's ignorant mistake. The young dandy had, as it happens, called on Gavrila Afanasevich the following day, wanting to apologize, but his mannerisms did not impress the proud boyar, who wittily dubbed him "a French monkey."[30]

It was a feast day. Gavrila Afanasevich was expecting a number of relatives and friends. A long table was being laid for dinner, in the old hall. The guests arrived with their wives and daughters, now liberated from the confines of their homes by the decrees of the sovereign and by his own example. Natalya Gavrilovna went up to each guest in turn, carrying a silver tray of golden goblets of wine; the men drank, each regretting that the kiss once bestowed with the wine was now out of fashion. Then they sat down at table. The place of honor, beside Gavrila Afanasevich, was taken by his father-in-law, Prince Boris Alexeyevich Lykov, a boyar of about seventy. The other guests took their seats in accordance with family seniority, thus paying homage to the happy times when the order of precedence was inviolable.[31] Men sat on one side, women on the other. At the end, in their usual places, sat the elderly housekeeper in her old-fashioned cloak and headdress;[32] the dwarf, a tiny woman of about thirty, prim and wrinkled; and the captive Swede in his worn blue uniform. Surrounding the table, which was laid with dishes of every sort, was a crowd of solicitous servants; among them was the butler, conspicuous by his severe gaze, his fine paunch, and his imperious immobility. At first, all attention was concentrated on the products of our traditional cuisine; the general silence was interrupted only by the sound of busy spoons ringing against plates. Then the host sensed that it was time to engage his guests in pleasant conversation, and so he turned around and said, "But where's Yekimovna? Call her at once." This sent servants rushing in different directions—but at that very moment an old woman came in, humming and doing a little dance. Her face was plastered with white lead and rouge; and she was wearing a low-cut damask round gown,[33] decked in flowers and spangles. Her arrival was greeted with evident pleasure.

"Greetings, Yekimovna," said Prince Lykov. "How are you keeping?"

"I'm keepin' grand, cousin dear—singin', dancin', awaitin' the man who'll beg for my hand."

"Where, my fool, have you been?" asked Gavrila Afanasevich.

"Why, dressin' up, cousin, as the Germans do—for the sake of our guests, for the sake of God's feast, at the tsar's behest, as the boyars think best, on your behalf, to make the world laugh."

Everyone laughed loudly, and the fool took her place behind the host's chair.

"The fool lies and lies—and out comes the truth," said Tatyana Afanasyevna, Gavrila's elder sister, whom he loved and respected. "The fashions these days, they really do make the world laugh. Of course, when you men are shaving off your beards[34] and putting on skimpy kaftans, what right have we to complain? Still, I do miss our old cotton *sarafans* and headdresses, and the ribbons young girls used to wear in their hair. I mean, you look at one of today's beauties and you don't know whether to laugh or cry! Hair like a bundle of tow, whipped up, greased all over, and sprinkled with French flour... Belly laced in so tight, you're afraid the girl will snap in half! Skirt draped over hoops, so she has to squeeze sideways into a carriage. And to go through a door she has to bend double. Can't stand, can't sit, can't even breathe—the poor darlings are martyrs!"

"My dear Tatyana Afanasyevna," said Kirila Petrovich T., the former military commander of Ryazan, where he had acquired, by fair means or foul, three thousand serfs and a young wife, "if you ask me, a wife can dress however she pleases—like a scarecrow, like a Chinese emperor—just as long as she doesn't order new dresses every month and throw away clothes she's only worn once. In the old days, a grandmother's *sarafan* was a granddaughter's dowry. Now it's the mistress's *robe ronde* one day, and a serf's the next. What's to be done? It's a tragedy. It's the ruin of our old Russian nobility." He sighed and glanced at his wife, Maria Ilinichna. She did not appear to be enjoying either his praise of the past or his censure of the present. Other beauties at the table seemed to feel the same, but they remained silent, for in those times modesty was considered an indispensable attribute of a young lady.[35]

"And who's to blame, I ask you?" said Gavrila Afanasevich, filling a cup with frothing mead.[36] "We ourselves, don't you think? Young women make fools of themselves, and we indulge them."

"But what's to be done?" Kirila Petrovich repeated. "The matter's out of our hands. Some of us would be only too glad to lock our wives in their chambers, but what about the assemblies? Our women get drummed to the palace! You're about to give your wife a whipping, and there she is, putting on her new attire... It's these damned assemblies! I tell you, they're the Lord's punishment for our sins..."[37]

Maria Ilinichna was itching to speak. Unable to contain herself, she turned to her husband with a sour smile and asked what possible harm could come from the assemblies.

"What harm, eh?" Kirila Petrovich retorted. "Ever since the assemblies started, husbands and wives have ceased to live in harmony. Women have forgotten the words of the apostle: 'Let the wife see that she reverence her husband.'[38] They no longer think about their households—only about new dresses. Instead of doing what's right by their husbands, they flirt with giddy young officers. Do you think it seemly, madam, for a Russian noblewoman to be rubbing elbows with German tobacco merchants and the women who work for them?[39] Or to be prancing and prattling with young men late into the night! With young men they don't know at all—who aren't even related to them!"

"I have a word for your ear, but the wolf is near," said Gavrila Afanasevich, with an anxious frown.[40] "Still, I must confess—I've no great love of these assemblies myself. Before you know it, you're accosted by some drunkard. Or else they compel you to drink too much yourself and turn you into a laughingstock. Or some scapegrace takes liberties with your daughter... Young men these days are spoiled beyond all bounds. Why, only the other night, at the last assembly, the son of the late Yevgraf Sergeyevich Korsakov made a real spectacle of himself with my Natasha. I can tell you, I saw red. The next day I see someone driving right into my yard, and I wonder: Who has God brought my way? Could it be Prince Alexander Danilovich? No such luck! It's that young knave again, Ivan Yevgrafovich... And did he have the manners to stop at the gate, get out, and walk up to the front door? Not likely! And so in he flew—and there he was, bowing, scraping, and chatter, chatter, chatter. You should see my fool Yekimovna imitate him. It'll make you split your sides...Yes, come here, fool, and show us that monkey from over the water."

Yekimovna snatched the lid from one of the dishes, tucked it under her arm as if it were a hat, and began to bow, scrape, and grimace to all sides, mumbling, "Mees*you*...Mam*zel*...assemb*lay*...par*dohn*." The guests laughed and laughed.

"Korsakov to a T," said old Prince Lykov, wiping away tears of laughter while everyone slowly calmed down. "But there's no getting away from it. He's neither the first nor the last to return to holy Russia from those godless German lands as a complete buffoon. What do our lads learn there? To bow and scrape, to chatter in God knows what tongues, to disrespect their elders and chase after other men's wives. God help me, but of all our young men educated in far-off lands, the only one who's the least like a human being is the tsar's African."

"You're quite right," said Gavrila Afanasevich. "He's a steady, decent fellow, not like that weathercock Korsakov... Now who's that driving through the gate? Surely it's not that foreign monkey again?" He turned to the servants. "Look sharp, you lazy beasts—get out there and send him packing! And tell him never..."

"Are you mad, graybeard, or just blind?" Yekimovna broke in. "Can't you see? It's the sovereign's sleigh. It's the tsar!"

Gavrila Afanasevich leaped to his feet. Everyone rushed to the windows and, indeed, saw the sovereign—leaning on the shoulder of his orderly as he mounted the steps. The house was thrown into confusion. Gavrila Afanasevich hurried out to meet Peter; dazed servants rushed to and fro; the guests took fright, and some even wondered about possible paths of escape. But then Peter's voice thundered out in the anteroom; everything went still, and the tsar walked in, accompanied by Gavrila Afanasevich, now dumbfounded with joy. "Greetings, ladies and gentlemen," said Peter, smiling genially. All bowed low. The tsar glanced quickly round the room, looking for his host's young daughter. He beckoned to her. Natalya Gavrilovna got to her feet. She walked over to Peter without hesitation, although she was blushing not only from ear to ear but even down to her shoulders. "You grow prettier with each hour," Peter said to her. As was his way, he kissed her on the top of the head. Then he turned to the guests. "Well, then—it seems I've disturbed you. You were having dinner. Carry on. Go back to your seats. As for me—I'll have some anise vodka, Gavrila Afanasevich." Gavrila rushed over to the majestic butler, snatched the tray from his hands, filled a little golden goblet with vodka, and held it out to the sovereign with a bow. Peter drank the vodka, bit into a pretzel, and again urged the guests to return to their dinner. Everyone went back to their former places, except for the dwarf and the housekeeper, who did not dare to remain at a table graced by the tsar's presence. Peter sat down beside Gavrila Afanasevich and asked for a bowl of cabbage soup. His orderly then handed him a wooden spoon inlaid with ivory, and a knife and fork with bone handles painted green; Peter always used his own cutlery. The meal, only a few minutes earlier so merry and lively, continued in silent restraint. Gavrila Afanasevich, out of both joy and a sense of deference, ate nothing at all. The other guests followed suit, listening reverently as the sovereign and the Swedish captive spoke in German about the 1701 campaign. The fool, whom the sovereign addressed several times, answered with a stiff timidity that (I note in passing) cast doubt on the reality of her foolishness.

At last the meal came to an end. The sovereign rose first, followed by the guests. Saying, "Gavrila Afanasevich, I must speak to you in private," he took his host by the arm, led him into the drawing room, and closed the door behind them. The guests remained in the dining room, whispering about what might have prompted this unexpected visit. For fear of appearing indiscreet, they began to go their separate ways, one by one, without thanking their host for his hospitality.[41] Gavrila Afanasevich's father-in-law, daughter, and sister saw each guest quietly to the threshold—and then remained alone in the dining room, waiting for the sovereign to emerge.

5

Either I am not a miller
Or you'll have a wife by dinner.
                    —ABLESIMOV, in the opera *The Miller*[42]

AFTER half an hour the door opened, and Peter appeared. He answered the bows of Prince Lykov, Tatyana Afanasyevna, and Natalya with a dignified nod, then went straight out into the anteroom. Gavrila Afanasevich handed the sovereign his red sheepskin coat, saw him to his sleigh, and thanked him for the honor of this visit. Peter set off.

Gavrila Afanasevich came back to the dining room, looking preoccupied. He tersely ordered the servants to clear the table, sent Natalya to her room, told his sister and father-in-law that he needed to speak with them, and led them into the bedchamber where he usually rested after dinner. The old prince stretched himself out on the oak bed, while Tatyana sat in an old-fashioned damask armchair, resting her feet on a small stool. Gavrila closed all the doors, sat down on the bed by the prince's feet, and said, in a low voice, "The sovereign did not come here for nothing... Guess what he wished to discuss?"

"How are we to know, Brother?" replied Tatyana.

"Has the tsar appointed you commander of some military district?" asked the prince. "God knows, it's high time. Or did he offer you an ambassadorship? That isn't only a job for clerks, you know—boyars get sent to foreign sovereigns too."

"No," Gavrila replied, frowning. "I'm a gentleman of the old school. Our service is no longer needed... Although a Russian Orthodox boyar may be worth all today's upstarts, pie vendors,[43] and heathens put together—but that's another story..."

"So what kept the two of you talking so long, Brother?" asked Tatyana. "Don't tell me some misfortune has befallen you—God forbid and have mercy!"

"Not exactly—but I can't deny that I feel troubled."

"What is it, Brother? What's the matter?"

"It has to do with Natasha. The tsar wishes to arrange her marriage."

"The Lord be praised!" said Tatyana, crossing herself. "The girl's of the right age—and a fine matchmaker means a fine suitor! God grant them love and good counsel—and we are indeed honored. But who does the tsar have in mind?"

"Huh..." grunted Gavrila. "Who indeed?"

"Who indeed?" repeated the prince, who was already dozing off.

"Guess," said Gavrila.

"How, dear Brother?" replied Tatyana. "How can we? There are more than enough young men at court. Any one of them would be happy to make your Natasha his own. Could it be Dolgoruky?"

"No, it's not Dolgoruky."

"Well, that's a blessing. He's proud as a peacock. Is it Shein, then? Or Troyekurov?"[44]

"No, neither of them."

"Well, that too is no loss. A pair of weathercocks, with too many German airs about them. Miloslavsky?"

"No."

"That's no loss either. Rich, but stupid. Yeletsky, then? Lvov? Or perhaps Raguzinsky? No, I've no idea. Whom does the tsar wish Natasha to marry?"

"The blackamoor Ibrahim."

Tatyana gasped and threw up her hands. The prince raised his head from the pillows and repeated in astonishment, "The blackamoor Ibrahim!"

"Dearest Brother," Tatyana pleaded tearfully, "do not destroy your dear child. Do not let Natasha fall into the clutches of that black devil."

"But how am I to refuse the sovereign?" replied Gavrila. "Moreover, he's promised to show us—all of us—his especial favor."

"But how can we?" exclaimed the old prince, now very much awake. "How can we marry Natasha, my dear granddaughter, to a blackamoor who's been bought and sold?"[45]

"He's no commoner," answered Gavrila. "He's the son of a blackamoor sultan. Infidels took him captive and offered him for sale in Constantinople. Our ambassador redeemed him, then presented him as a gift to the tsar. The blackamoor's eldest brother came to Russia with a large ransom and—"

"Brother dear," Tatyana interrupted, "we've all heard the fairy tale about Prince Bova and Yeruslan Lazarevich. Just tell us how you answered the sovereign!"[46]

"I said that we lie in his power, and that it is our bounden duty to obey him in all things."[47]

At that moment there was a noise just outside. Gavrila went to open the door. Sensing resistance, he pushed harder. The door opened—and there lay Natalya, in a swoon. There was blood on the floor.

Her heart had sunk when the sovereign first locked himself up with her father. She had sensed that all this had something to do with her. And when Gavrila sent her away, saying he needed to speak to her aunt and grandfather, she could not resist the pull of feminine curiosity. She crept quietly through the inner rooms to the door of the bedchamber and overheard every word of their terrible conversation. On hearing how her father replied to the tsar, the poor girl had lost her senses, collapsed, and hit her head on the iron-hooped chest that held her dowry.

The servants came running. They lifted Natalya from the floor, carried her to her chamber, and laid her on the bed. After some time, she came to. She opened her eyes but was unable to recognize either her father or her aunt. Now in a high fever, she began to rave about the tsar's blackamoor and about the wedding—and then, in a mournful, piercing voice, cried out, "Valerian, dearest Valerian, my life! Save me! They're coming for me!"

Tatyana looked anxiously at her brother, who turned pale, bit his lip, and left the room without a word. He went back down to the old prince, who was unable to climb the stairs.

"How is she?" asked the prince.

"Not good," replied the vexed father. "Worse than I expected: she's delirious, raving about Valerian."

"Who on earth is Valerian?" the old prince asked in alarm. "You don't mean that orphan, the rebel's son you brought up in your own home?"[48]

"The very one," answered Gavrila. "His father saved my life during the uprising, and the devil drove me to take the damned wolf cub into my house. Two years ago I did as he asked and got him into a regiment. Natasha burst into tears as she bid him farewell, while he stood there as if turned to stone. I didn't like the look of all that, and I remember talking about it to my sister . . . But Natasha hasn't mentioned him since, and he hasn't sent us so much as a word himself. I thought she'd forgotten all about him. Evidently not. So that's that: she must marry the blackamoor."

It would have been in vain to protest. Prince Lykov went back home. Tatyana remained at Natalya's bedside. Gavrila sent for the doctor, then locked himself in his room. A gloomy calm settled upon the house.

The tsar's unexpected matchmaking had surprised Ibrahim at least as much as it did Gavrila Afanasevich. One day, as the two of them were working together, Peter had said to Ibrahim, "You look down in the mouth, my boy. Be honest with me now: Is there anything that you need?"

Ibrahim had assured the sovereign that he was content with his lot and wanted nothing better.

"Well, if nothing's seriously wrong," Peter had replied, "if it's a mere fit of melancholy, I know what will cheer you up."

After they'd finished their work, Peter asked Ibrahim, "What do you reckon to the young lady you danced the minuet with at the assembly?"

"She's very sweet, sire, and she seems kind and modest."

"Good—then I'll introduce you right away. Would you like to marry her?"

"Marry her, sire? Me?"

"Listen, Ibrahim, you're all alone here, without kith or kin. You're a stranger to everyone but myself. If I should die today, what would become of you, my poor African? You need to establish yourself while there's still time, to find support in new connections. You need to ally with the Russian boyars."

"Sire, I am happy under the patronage of your majesty. God forbid that I should outlive my tsar and benefactor. I want nothing more. But even if I did have it in mind to marry, would the young lady and her family agree? My looks—"

"Your looks? What nonsense! You're as good-looking as anyone. Anyway, a young girl must obey her parents. And as for old Gavrila Afanasevich...There's not much he can say if *I* show up as your matchmaker!"

The sovereign ordered his sleigh and set off, leaving Ibrahim deep in thought.

"Marriage?" he said to himself. "But why not? Must I live out my days in loneliness, ignorant of man's greatest joys and most sacred duties, simply because I was born beneath the fifteenth parallel? I cannot hope to be loved—but that's neither here nor there. Who can truly believe in love? Can such a thing even exist in the fickle heart of a woman? Having rejected, once and for all, such charming delusions, I now have my eye on more substantial charms. The sovereign is right: I must secure my future. By marrying the Rzhevsky girl, I shall join the proud Russian nobility and cease to be a stranger in my new fatherland. I shall not demand love from my wife, only that she be faithful. And I shall win her friendship through constant tenderness, trust, and indulgence."[49]

Ibrahim would have liked, as was his way, to keep on with his work, but his imagination was now too excited. He abandoned his papers and went out for a walk by the Neva. Suddenly he heard Peter's voice. He turned around and saw the sovereign walking towards him, with a smile on his face.

"That's it, my boy," Peter said, taking Ibrahim by the arm. "I've arranged everything. Pay your father-in-law a visit tomorrow. Be sure to flatter his boyar pride. Leave your sleigh at the gate. Walk through his courtyard on foot. Dwell on his merits, on his noble lineage—he'll be enchanted. And now," he went on, shaking his oak cudgel, "take me to that swindler Menshikov. I'll make him pay for his latest devilry."

Ibrahim thanked Peter, from the bottom of his heart, for his fatherly solicitude, accompanied him to Prince Menshikov's magnificent palace, and then made his way home.

6

A LAMP was burning quietly before the glass-fronted icon case, lighting the gold and silver of the family's ancient icons. Its weak, quivering flame illuminated a curtained bed and a small table, on which stood a number of labeled phials. Beside the stove, a maid was sitting at a spinning wheel, and only the murmur of her spindle interrupted the silence.

"Who is it?" asked a feeble voice.

The maid got to her feet, went over to the bed, and gently lifted the curtain.

"Will it soon be morning?" asked Natalya.

"Already noon, miss," answered the maid.

"Good Lord, why's it so dark?"

"Windows are shuttered, miss."

"Quick, help me get dressed."

"Not allowed, miss—doctor's orders."

"Am I ill? How long have I—?"

"Been two weeks, miss."

"How come? It seems I only lay down yesterday…"

Natalya fell silent, trying to collect her scattered thoughts. Something had happened to her—but what? She couldn't remember. The maid stood by the bed, awaiting her orders. Then they heard muffled sounds from the floor below.

"What was that?" asked Natalya.

"Masters must've finished eating," answered the maid. "Getting up from the table. Tatyana Afanasyevna will be coming up now."

This seemed to gladden Natalya. She waved her feeble hand. The maid drew the bed-curtain and sat down again behind her spinning wheel.

A few minutes later a head in a broad white bonnet with dark ribbons appeared at the door and a quiet voice asked, "How is my Natasha?"

"Hello, Auntie!" the patient said quietly.

Tatyana hurried over to the bed.

"The miss is in her right mind again," said the maid, carefully drawing up an armchair.

The old woman, with tears in her eyes, kissed the pale, languid face of her niece and sat down beside her. The German doctor, in his black kaftan and learned wig, followed Tatyana into the room; he took Natalya's pulse and declared, first in Latin and then in Russian, that the girl was now out of danger. He asked for paper and ink, wrote out a new prescription, and then left. Tatyana rose from her armchair, gave Natalya another kiss, and went straight downstairs to share the good news.

Sitting in the drawing room was the tsar's African. Hat in hand, wearing sword and uniform, he was conversing quietly and deferentially with Gavrila Afanasevich. Korsakov was lounging on the down-filled divan, listening absentmindedly and teasing a venerable old borzoi. Wearying of this, he went up to the mirror—his usual refuge during moments of idleness—and in it glimpsed Tatyana Afanasyevna. She was signaling to her brother from behind the door.

"Gavrila Afanasevich, you're being summoned," said Korsakov, interrupting Ibrahim in mid-sentence. Gavrila at once went to join his sister and closed the door behind him.

"I marvel at your patience," Korsakov said to Ibrahim. "You've been listening to the man's twaddle about the antiquity of the Lykovs and Rzhevskys for a solid hour, and you've even chimed in with edifying comments of your own. In your place, *j'aurais planté là* the old liar and all his kin, including your dear Natasha, that *petite santé* of a malingerer... Be honest with me: Are you really in love with that little *mijaurée*?[50] Ibrahim, please follow my advice just this once—my head is screwed on straighter than it appears. Abandon your silly plan. Don't get married. I don't think your bride-to-be has any particular liking for you. And in this world, anything may happen! For instance, I'm quite good-looking, of course, but I can assure you that some of the husbands I've deceived are no less good-looking. And you yourself... don't you remember our Parisian friend, Count D.? A woman's fidelity cannot be relied on. Happy is he who accepts this with equanimity. But you! With your ardent, brooding, and suspicious nature, your flattened nose and puffy lips, and that wild, woolly hair—how can you throw yourself into all the perils of married life?"[51]

"I thank you for your friendly advice," Ibrahim cut in coldly, "but you know the old saying: 'No need to rock the cradle of another's sorrow...'"

"Careful, Ibrahim!" Korsakov replied with a laugh. "Or you might have to prove the wisdom of those words all too literally."

Meanwhile, the voices in the other room were becoming heated.

"You'll be the death of her!" Tatyana was saying. "She'll drop dead at the sight of him."

"But judge for yourself," retorted her stubborn brother. "The young man has been visiting us for the last two weeks, and he still hasn't set eyes on his fiancée. He may end up thinking that her illness is a sham, that we're only playing for time, trying to think of some way to rid ourselves of him. And what about the tsar? He's already inquired three times after Natasha's health. Say what you like, but I, for one, have no wish to quarrel with the tsar."

"Heavens!" said Tatyana. "What will become of our poor girl? At the very least, let me prepare her—"

Gavrila agreed and returned to the drawing room. "Thank the Lord," he said to Ibrahim. "Natasha is out of danger. If I weren't ashamed to leave our dear Korsakov down here by himself, I would take you upstairs to see your fiancée this minute."

Korsakov congratulated Gavrila, said he could look after himself, that he absolutely had to be on his way—and dashed out into the anteroom, not even allowing his host to see him to the door.

Tatyana had hurried upstairs, intending to prepare her niece for the visitor she so dreaded. Struggling to get her breath back, she had sat down beside Natalya's bed and grasped her hand, but before she could say a word the door opened. "Who is it?" asked Natalya. Tatyana froze. Gavrila drew back the curtain, looked at his daughter coldly, and asked her how she was feeling. The young woman wanted to smile at her father, but she couldn't; she was too disturbed by his stern gaze. Then she thought she could see someone else, standing beside her father. With an effort, she raised her head—and recognized the tsar's African. Suddenly she remembered everything. Her future appeared before her in all its horror. Her wan face showed no visible shock, but her head fell back on the pillow and she closed her eyes. Her heart was now beating feverishly. Tatyana gestured to her brother that the girl needed to sleep, and everyone quietly left, except for the maid, who sat down again at her spinning wheel.

The unfortunate beauty opened her eyes. Seeing that she was alone, she asked the maid to summon the dwarf. But that very moment the dear little poppet rolled like a ball right up to her bed. Sparrow (as she was called) had raced up the stairs after Gavrila and Ibrahim as fast as her stubby legs would carry her. She had then hidden behind the door, true to the curiosity native to the fair sex. Natalya sent the maid away, and Sparrow sat down on a stool beside the bed.

Never had so tiny a body been invested with such an excess of mental energy. Sparrow stuck her nose into everything and was privy to everything—there was nothing that was not her concern. Her wily, ingratiating mind had won for her the love of her masters and the hatred of the entire household, over which she ruled like a despot. Gavrila Afanasevich listened to her denunciations, complaints, and petty pleas; Tatyana constantly solicited her opinions and followed her advice; and Natalya's affection for her knew no bounds. She confided to her her every thought, every movement of her sixteen-year-old heart.

"Sparrow, have you heard?" she asked. "Father wants to marry me off to the African."

The dwarf heaved a deep sigh, and her wrinkled face wrinkled still more.

"Is there really no hope?" continued Natasha. "Won't Father take pity on me?"

The dwarf shook her capped head.

"Won't Auntie or Grandad take my side?"

"No, miss. While you were ill, the African enchanted them all. The master is mad about him, the prince can talk of no one else, and Tatyana Afanasyevna says it's a pity he's an African, as we couldn't have wished for a better bridegroom."

"My God, my God!" moaned poor Natalya.

"It isn't so bad, my pretty," said the dwarf, kissing her limp hand. "It may be your lot to marry the African, but you'll still be a free woman. Things have changed since the old days. Husbands no longer lock up their wives. I hear the African is rich. Your home will be a full chalice—you'll live in clover..."

"Poor Valerian," said Natalya, speaking so quietly that the dwarf could only guess at her words.

"That's just it, miss," Sparrow replied, lowering her voice conspiratorially. "If only you'd thought less about that son of a rebel, you wouldn't have raved about him in your fever, and the master wouldn't have become so angry."

"What!" Natalya exclaimed. "I raved about Valerian? And Father heard? And now he's angry?"

"All too true," said the dwarf. "And now, if you tell him you don't want to marry the African, he'll blame it on Valerian. There's nothing you can do. You must submit to your father. And whatever will be, will be."

Natalya did not reply. Her heart's innermost secret had been exposed to her father—that was all she could think of. Only one hope remained: that she might die before this hateful marriage. This thought brought her comfort. Weak and dejected, she resigned herself to her fate.

7

IN GAVRILA Afanasevich's home, to the right of the entrance room,[52] was a cramped space with one small window. In it stood a simple bed covered with a flannel blanket, and a small spruce table. An open music book lay on the table, beside a lit tallow candle. On the wall hung an old blue uniform and an equally old three-cornered cocked hat. Above the hat, held in place by three nails, was a crude engraving of Charles XII on horseback. This humble abode was filled with the sounds of a flute. In his nightgown and nightcap, the captive dancing-master, the room's solitary resident, was relieving the boredom of a winter evening by playing old Swedish marches, which reminded him of the cheerful days of his youth. After devoting two whole hours to this exercise, the Swede took his flute apart, placed it in its case, and began to undress.

Just then he heard the latch on his door being lifted. A tall, handsome young man in uniform came in.

The startled Swede got to his feet.

"You don't recognize me, Gustav Adamych," the young visitor said in a voice full of emotion. "You don't remember the little boy whom you drilled like a Swedish soldier, with whom you almost set this very room ablaze, firing a child's cannon."

Gustav Adamych peered at him intently.

"Ja, ja!" he finally exclaimed, throwing his arms about the young man. "Vedy gud ... You are kom bak ... Sitt der, mine rascal, let oss talk."

Translated by Boris Dralyuk and Robert and Elizabeth Chandler

THE HISTORY OF THE VILLAGE
OF GORIUKHINO

IF GOD sends me readers, they may be curious to learn how it was that I resolved to write this history of the village of Goriukhino. To that end, I must go into a few preliminary details.

I was born of noble and honorable parents in the village of Goriukhino on 1 April 1801, and I received my primary education from our sexton. To this worthy gentleman I owe what later developed into a love of reading and of literary pursuits in general. My progress was slow but sound; by the age of ten I already knew almost everything that has remained until now in my memory—a memory that is weak by nature and which, on account of my equally frail health, I was not allowed to burden unnecessarily.

The calling of a man of letters has always seemed most enviable to me. My parents were respectable but straightforward people who had been brought up in accord with the old ways; they took no interest in reading and the only books to be found in the house were an ABC bought for me, some yearbooks, and Kurganov's *New Manual of Letter Writing*.[1] Reading the manual was for a long time the exercise I loved above all. Every day, even though I knew it by heart, I discovered in it new, previously unremarked beauties. After General Plemyannikov,[2] to whom my father had once been adjutant, Kurganov seemed to me the very greatest of men. I repeatedly inquired about him, but no one, sadly, was able to satisfy my curiosity. No one was personally acquainted with him and the only answer I received to my questions was that he was the author of the *New Manual*, a fact I already knew very well. Kurganov was like some ancient demigod, surrounded by the dark of obscurity; sometimes I doubted his very existence. His name, it seemed, was invented, and everything I had heard about him was a myth, awaiting the investigations of a new Niebuhr.[3] For all that, Kurganov continued to haunt my imagination. Wishing to attach some clear form to this mysterious figure, I finally decided he must resemble Koriuchkin the district assessor, a little old man with a red nose and flashing eyes.

In 1812 I was taken to Moscow and placed in Karl Ivanovich Meyer's boarding school, but in the end I spent only three months there. The school was closed when the enemy invaded, and I returned home. After the Twelve Nations[4] had been driven out, my parents wanted to take me to Moscow again to see if Karl Ivanovich had returned to his former hearth and home or—should they find only ashes—to enroll me in some other institution; but I begged my mother to allow me to stay in our country home, saying that my poor health did not permit me to rise at seven in the morning, as was the practice in all boarding schools. And so I reached the age of sixteen without progressing beyond my primary education; I spent my time playing ball with friends from the village, this being the only field of knowledge in which I had gained any proficiency during my months in the boarding school.

I then enlisted as a cadet in the —— Infantry Regiment, where I remained until this past year of 18—. My years of service left me with few pleasant memories: only those of being granted my commission, and of winning 245 rubles at cards on a day when I had only one ruble and sixty kopeks left in my pocket. Following the death of my dear parents, I was obliged to resign my commission and return to the family estate.

This period of my life is so important to me that I intend to write about it at some length, asking beforehand for my gracious reader's forgiveness if I abuse his indulgent attention.

It was a gloomy autumn day. When I reached the post station before the turning to Goriukhino, I hired a private coach and set off down the country road. Although I am placid by nature, I was so impatient to see the places where I had spent my happiest years that

I kept chivvying my coachman on, now promising him a tip, now threatening to hit him; and, it being simpler to poke him in the back than to take out and untie my purse, I must confess that I hit him two or three times, something that had never happened to me before, since for some reason I am especially fond of the estate of coachmen. The coachman urged his troika forward, but it seemed to me that, as coachmen often do, he was not only exhorting the horses and waving his whip in the air but also tightening the reins. At last I caught sight of the Goriukhino wood, and after another ten minutes we drove into the courtyard of the manor house. My heart was pounding. I looked around with feelings that are beyond words; it was eight years since I had last seen Goriukhino. Birch saplings once planted along the fence in my presence had grown into tall, spreading trees. The courtyard itself, once graced with three neat flowerbeds separated by broad sand-strewn paths, was now an unmowed meadow; a brown cow was grazing there. My *britchka*⁵ stopped by the front porch. My servant went to open the front door but found it boarded up, even though the shutters were open and the house looked inhabited. A woman came out of the servants' hut and asked whom I wanted to see. Learning who I was, she went back inside, and I was soon surrounded by household servants. The sight of so many faces—some long familiar, some new to me—and the exchange of many warm kisses was deeply affecting; I felt touched to the bottom of my heart. Boys I had played with were now grown men; girls who had once sat on the floor waiting to be sent on errands were married women. The men wept. To the women I said unceremoniously, "How you've aged!" "And how *you* have lost your looks, dear master!" they replied with feeling. They took me round to the back porch, where my old wet-nurse embraced me, weeping and sobbing as if I were some long-suffering Odysseus. Someone hurried off to light the stove in the bathhouse. The cook offered to prepare lunch for me—or, rather, supper, since it was already getting dark; from having nothing much to do, he had grown a beard. The rooms in which my former nurse and my late mother's maids had been living were quickly made ready for me. And so I found myself once again in my parents' humble abode; I fell asleep in the very room where, twenty-three years before, I had been born.

The next three weeks were taken up by a variety of tedious administrative tasks—dealing with assessors, marshals of the nobility, and all manner of provincial officials. At last I came into my inheritance and took possession of my patrimony. This brought me peace of mind, but the boredom of having nothing to do soon began to torment me. I was not yet acquainted with my kind and honorable neighbor ——. Managing an estate was an occupation quite alien to me. The conversation of my nurse, whom I had promoted to housekeeper and steward, consisted of precisely fifteen family stories. These were all of great interest but, since she always told them in exactly the same manner, she soon became for me another *New Manual of Letter Writing*; I knew the exact page on which I would find each sentence. As for the worthy manual itself, I found it in the storeroom, lying in a sorry state amid much clutter. I brought it out into the light and began to read, but Kurganov had lost his former appeal; I read through the manual once more and never opened it again.

In this extremity it occurred to me that I should, perhaps, endeavor to compose something myself.

The gentle reader already knows that I received a scant education and never had the opportunity to compensate for what I had missed; until the age of sixteen I played with boys from the village and after that I moved from province to province, from billet to billet, spending my time with Jews and sutlers, playing on shabby billiard tables and trudging through mud. Moreover, the calling of author seemed so problematic, so far beyond the reach of us amateurs, that the mere thought of taking up the pen was terrifying. Could I dare hope ever to count myself an author, when not even my burning desire to meet with an author had ever been granted? But this brings to mind an incident I must relate as evidence of my undying passion for our native letters.

In 1820, while I was still a cadet, official duties took me to Petersburg. I stayed for a week and, even though I knew no one there, I greatly enjoyed myself, slipping away every evening to the theater, to

the top balcony. I learned the names of all the actors and fell passionately in love with ——, who one Sunday played with great artistry
the role of Amalia in the drama *Misanthropy and Repentance*.[6] In the
morning, as I made my way back from the General Staff, I usually
went to a small coffee shop and read the literary journals over a cup
of hot chocolate. One day I was sitting there engrossed by a review
in *The Well-Intentioned*[7] when someone in a pea-colored coat came
up to my table and quietly pulled out a copy of the *Hamburg Gazette*
from beneath the pages I was reading. I was so absorbed that I did
not even look up at him. The stranger ordered a steak and sat down
opposite me. I went on reading, still paying him no attention. He
finished his lunch, scolded the waiter for his poor service, drank half
a bottle of wine, and left.

Two young people were eating there at the same time. "Do you
know who that was?" one of them said to the other. "It was Mr. B.,
the author."[8]

"Author!" I cried out involuntarily. Leaving my journal half read
and my chocolate half drunk, I rushed to pay my bill and, without
waiting for the change, dashed out onto the street. I looked all about
me, spotted the pea-colored coat in the distance, and set off, almost
at a run, along Nevsky Prospect. But after only a few steps I found
myself brought to a halt. I turned round—and a Guards officer pointed
out to me that, instead of pushing him off the pavement, I should
have stopped and stood to attention. After this reprimand I was more
cautious; but to my misfortune, I met more and more officers and
had to stop again and again, while the author continued to move
farther and farther away. Never had my soldier's greatcoat felt so
burdensome; never had I so longed for epaulettes. Not until the
Anichkin Bridge did I catch up with the pea-colored coat.

"Allow me to ask," I began, saluting, "whether you are the Mr. B.
whose excellent articles I have had the pleasure of reading in the
Champion of Enlightenment?"

"Certainly not, sir," he replied. "I am not an author but an advocate.
I do, however, know Mr. —— very well; I met him at the Police Bridge
only fifteen minutes ago."

Thus my esteem for Russian literature cost me thirty kopeks of lost change and a serious reprimand. I achieved nothing and was fortunate not to be arrested.

Against all the objections of my reason, the audacious idea of becoming a writer continued to haunt me. At last, no longer able to resist my natural inclinations, I stitched together a thick notebook, steadfastly resolved that I should fill every page one way or another. After analyzing and evaluating every genre of poetry (for I had not yet contemplated humble prose), I set my mind on composing an epic poem, on a theme taken from the history of our nation. It did not take me long to find a hero. I chose Rurik[9]—and got down to work.

I had acquired a certain proficiency in versification through transcribing the notebooks that had been passed around among us officers. These included poems such as "A Dangerous Neighbor,"[10] "A Critique of a Moscow Boulevard," "A Critique of the Presnya Ponds,"[11] and the like. In spite of this, my poem progressed only slowly, and I abandoned it at the third line. Concluding that the epic was not my genre, I began a tragedy about Rurik. The tragedy got nowhere.[12] I tried to turn it into a ballad, but that, too, seemed not to suit my talent. At last inspiration dawned on me: I began, and successfully completed, an inscription for a portrait of Rurik.

Even though my inscription was not altogether unworthy of note, especially as the first composition of a young versifier, I nevertheless came to feel that I had not been born a poet, and I contented myself with this first effort. But by now, through these creative endeavors, I had grown so attached to literary pursuits that I was unable to part with the notebook and the inkwell. I wanted to descend to prose.[13] At first, not wishing to burden myself with preparatory study, the elaboration of a plan, transitions between sections, and the like, I proposed to write down disparate thoughts, with no connection or order, in whatever form they presented themselves to me. Unfortunately, no thoughts at all came to mind. In the course of two days I composed only the following dictum: "He who does not obey the laws of reason and grows accustomed to following the promptings of passion will often err and condemn himself to later remorse."

This thought is indeed true, but it is far from new. Abandoning the idea of recording mere thoughts, I turned to the composition of stories but, being unpracticed in thinking up fictitious events, I selected a few notable anecdotes I had heard from people I knew; I tried to make truth beautiful by means of lively narration and, now and then, with the flowers of my own fancy. While setting down these stories, I gradually came to fashion a style of my own and learned to express myself correctly, pleasingly, and freely.[14] It was not long, however, before my stock of material ran out and I was once again seeking a subject for my literary activity.

The possibility of moving from trivial and questionable tales to the narration of true and great events had long stirred my imagination. A writer could achieve nothing higher, I believed, than to be the judge, observer, and prophet of peoples and epochs. But, given my pitiful education, what kind of history could I write? Diligent and learned scholars had gone before me. Was there any vein of history they had not yet exhausted? Should I attempt a universal history—as if the Abbé Millot had not already composed his immortal work?[15] If I turned to the history of my fatherland, what could I hope to add to Tatishchev, Boltin, and Golikov?[16] And was it likely that I, after failing even to master the Old Slavonic numerals, would prove able to delve into chronicles and divine the arcane meaning of a language now almost forgotten? I contemplated a history of lesser scope, such as that of our provincial capital—but even here I foresaw insurmountable obstacles. Traveling to the city, obligatory calls on the governor and the archbishop, requests for admission to archives and the repositories of monasteries, and the like. A history of our district town would have been more manageable, but neither philosopher nor pragmatic man of the world would have found it of interest; nor would such a history have provided sustenance for fine writing: it was not until 17— that —— was elevated to the status of town, and the only noteworthy event recorded in its chronicles is the terrible blaze that destroyed its marketplace and government buildings ten years ago.

A chance discovery resolved my uncertainties. While hanging up linen to dry in the attic, a servant woman found an old basket full of wood shavings, litter, and books. The entire household knew of my passion for reading. As I sat with my notebook, chewing my pen and wondering how best to compose a sermon to the villagers,[17] my housekeeper triumphantly dragged the basket into my room and exclaimed joyfully, "Books! Books!" "Books!" I repeated in rapture and rushed at the basket. There I found a whole heap of books in green and blue paper covers. It was, I realized, a collection of old yearbooks. This discovery dampened my enthusiasm, but I was still pleased with the unexpected find—they were, after all, books—and I rewarded the washerwoman's zeal generously, with a silver half-ruble. Once I was alone again, I began to examine my yearbooks and was soon deeply engrossed. They formed an unbroken series, precisely fifty-five years from 1744 to 1799. The sheets of blue paper usually bound into such yearbooks were covered from top to bottom in old-fashioned handwriting. As I cast an eye over these lines, I was astonished to find that they contained not only household accounts and observations about the weather but also brief items of historical information about the village of Goriukhino. I lost no time in setting about a complete analysis of these precious notes, and I soon established that they constituted a full history of my ancestral estate for the best part of a century, in the strictest chronological order. Moreover, they furnished an inexhaustible store of economical, statistical, meteorological, and other scientific observations. From that day, I devoted myself exclusively to the study of these notes, understanding that it might be possible to extract from them a shapely, interesting, and instructive narrative. Once I had sufficiently familiarized myself with these precious memorials, I began casting about for new sources for the history of the village of Goriukhino. And the abundance of such sources soon came to astound me. After devoting a full six months to preliminary study, I at last got down to the labor I had so long looked forward to and with God's help completed it on this 3rd day of November, 1827.[18]

Now that I have reached the end of my difficult task, I shall lay down my pen and—like a certain fellow historian whose name escapes me[19]—wander sadly into my garden to reflect on what I have accomplished. To me, too, it seems that the world no longer needs me. *The History of Goriukhino* has been written; I have fulfilled my duty, and it is time for me to go to my rest!

Here I append a list of the sources that have served me during the composition of *The History of Goriukhino*:

1. A collection of old yearbooks, in fifty-four issues. The first twenty issues are covered with writing in an old-fashioned hand, with Old Church Slavonic abbreviations. This chronicle was composed by my great-grandfather Andrey Stepanovich Belkin. It is notable for its clarity and concision of style.[20] For example:

> May 4th. Snow. Trishka thrashed for rudeness.
> 6th. The dun cow died. Senka thrashed for drunkenness.
> 8th. Clear skies.
> 9th. Rain and snow. Trishka thrashed on account of the weather.
> 11th. Clear skies. Fresh snow. Shot three hares.

And so on, with no reflections. The remaining thirty-five issues include entries in a variety of hands, mostly in what is called the shopkeeper's script, with or without abbreviations; the entries are wordy, disconnected, and show little regard for orthography. Here and there the writing is that of a woman. Among these entries are some by my grandfather, Ivan Andreyevich Belkin, others by my grandmother (his wife), Yevpraxia Alexeyevna, and still others by the steward Garbovitsky.

2. A chronicle written by the Goriukhino sexton. I discovered this intriguing manuscript at the house of my parish priest, who is married to the chronicler's daughter. Its first pages had been torn out and used by the priest's children to make paper kites. One such kite landed in the middle of my courtyard. I picked it up and was about to return

it to the children when I noticed that it was covered in writing. From the first lines I could see that the kite had been fashioned from a chronicle; by good fortune, I was able to rescue the remaining pages. This chronicle, which I then acquired in exchange for a quarter-measure of oats, is distinguished by its profundity of thought and unusual magniloquence.

3. Oral traditions. I did not scorn any source of information. But I am especially indebted to Agrafena Trifonova, the mother of Avdey the village elder and reputed to have been the mistress of Garbovitsky the steward.

4. Census registers (and income and expenditure ledgers), with notes by former village elders on the mores and living conditions of the peasants.

The land known by the name of its capital Goriukhino takes up well over six hundred acres of the earth's surface. Its population amounts to sixty-three souls. To the north it borders on the territory of the villages of Deriukhovo and Perkukhovo, whose inhabitants are poor, scrawny, and short of stature, but whose proud owners are devoted to the martial exercise of the hare hunt. To the south side, the River Sivka separates Goriukhino from the lands of the Karachevo free-holders[21]—restless neighbors notorious for their unbridled cruelty. Bounding it to the west are the flourishing fields of Zakharino, thriving under the sway of wise and enlightened landowners. To the east, it adjoins wild uninhabited country, an impassable bog where only cranberries grow, where the only sound is the monotonous croak of frogs, and which an old superstition holds to be the abode of a certain demon.

(N.B. This bog is indeed called Demon's Bog. It is said that a half-witted woman used to tend a herd of swine not far from this isolated spot. She became pregnant and could provide no satisfactory explanation for this. Popular belief held the bog demon responsible, but this tale is not worthy of the attention of a historian, and after Niebuhr it would be inexcusable to give credence to it.)[22]

From ancient times Gorokhino[23] has been famed for its fertility and favorable climate. Rye, oats, barley, and buckwheat all grow on its rich fields. A birch wood and a fir forest supply its inhabitants with timber and fallen branches for the construction and heating of their dwellings. There is no shortage of hazelnuts, cranberries, whortleberries, and bilberries. Mushrooms are unusually plentiful; baked with sour cream they make a tasty, though unwholesome, dish. The pond teems with carp, and pike and burbot are to be found in the River Sivka.

The male inhabitants of Goriukhino are mostly of middling height and a sturdy build, with gray eyes and fair or reddish hair. The women are noted for their snub noses, prominent cheekbones, and ample proportions. (N.B. The expression "strapping wench" occurs frequently in the elder's notes to the census registers.) The men are of good character, hardworking (especially on their own strip of land), brave, and combative: many of them have fought bears single-handed and are renowned throughout the district as fist-fighters. By and large, they are partial to the sensual delights of drunkenness. On top of their household tasks, the women share a large part of their men's labors; and they do not yield to them in courage, few of them showing any fear of the village elder. Known as spearbearers (derived from the word "spear"), they constitute a powerful civil guard that watches untiringly over the courtyard of the manor house.[24] The spearbearers' chief duty is to beat a stone against an iron plate as often as possible, to ward off evil-doing. They are as chaste as they are beautiful; they respond sternly and spiritedly to the advances of the insolent.

The natives have long conducted a flourishing trade in bast, bast baskets, and bast shoes. This trade is facilitated by the River Sivka, which in spring they cross in dugouts, like the ancient Scandinavians, and which at other times of the year they wade across, after rolling their trousers up to their knees.

The tongue of Goriukhino is undoubtedly a branch of the Slavonic family, but it is as distinct from it as Russian itself. It abounds in short forms and truncations; some letters have been entirely eliminated from it, or else replaced by others. Nevertheless, a Great Russian can easily understand a Goriukhinite, and vice versa.

As a rule, the men used to get married in their thirteenth year to maidens aged around twenty. For four or five years, the wives would beat their husbands. After this the husbands would start to beat their wives. Thus each sex enjoyed its period of power, and equilibrium was maintained.

Funerals were conducted as follows: the deceased was carried out to the cemetery on the day of his death, so that he would not take up space in the hut to no purpose. This led to a few occasions when, to the indescribable joy of his family, the dead man would sneeze or yawn just as he was being taken in his coffin across the village boundary. More often, though, wives would weep and wail for their husbands, repeating, "O light of my life, o my brave one! Whom have you abandoned me to? How shall I honor your memory?" When all had returned from the cemetery, the wake would begin, and friends and relatives would be drunk for two or three days on end, or even for an entire week—depending on their zeal and the degree of their attachment to the memory of the deceased. These ancient rites have been preserved to this day.

The Goriukhinites' apparel consisted of a long shirt worn over trousers, a clear indication of their Slavonic origins.[25] In winter they wore sheepskin coats, but more for show than out of real need, since they usually just flung them over one shoulder and discarded them altogether when undertaking any task that required even the slightest movement.

Poetry and the arts and sciences have flourished in Goriukhino since the earliest times. In addition to the priest and deacons, the village has always harbored scholars. The annals mention a clerk by the name of Terenty, who lived circa 1767, and who could write not only with his right hand but also with his left. This unusual man was famed throughout the district for the composition of all kinds of letters, petitions, and special passports. Having suffered more than once for his art, for his readiness to oblige and take part in various events of note,[26] he finally died at a ripe old age, just as he was learning to write with his right foot, since by then the script of both his hands had become all too well known. As the reader will soon see, this man played an important role in the history of the village.

Music has always been the favored art of the more educated Gorokhinites. To this day, balalaikas and bagpipes, delighting the sensitive heart, can be heard throughout the village, especially in the ancient public building adorned with a fir tree and the image of a two-headed eagle.[27]

Poetry, too, once flourished in ancient Goriukhino. To this day the verses of Arkhip the Bald remain in the memory of posterity. In tenderness they are in no way inferior to the eclogues of the celebrated Virgil, and in beauty of imagination they far surpass the eclogues of Mr. Sumarokov.[28] And though they cannot compete with the latest productions of our Muses with regard to intricacy of style, they are equal to them in ingenuity and wit.

Let me, as an example, quote this satirical poem:

> Once a month the village elder
> Shows his tallies to the squire.
> How he tallies up them tallies
> Our squire he don't inquire.
> Anton pillages the peasants
> And he steals from the squire.
> Anton's wife parades around,
> Showing off her grand attire.

Having thus acquainted the reader with the ethnographical and statistical realities of Goriukhino, let me now move on to the narrative proper.

LEGENDARY TIMES
Trifon the Village Elder

Goriukhino's form of government has changed several times. It has been in turn under the rule of elders chosen by the village commune, of stewards appointed by the landowner, and of the landowners themselves. I will consider the advantages and disadvantages of these different forms of government in the course of my narrative.

The foundation of Goriukhino and its first settlement are covered by the dark of obscurity. According to legend, Goriukhino was once a large and wealthy village. The quitrent was collected just once a year and sent off, to persons unrecorded, in several carts. In those days everything could be bought cheaply and sold for a good price. Stewards did not exist, village elders did not mistreat anyone, the peasants worked little yet lived without a care, and even the shepherds wore boots while tending their flocks. We should not let this charming picture delude us. The idea of a golden age is shared by all mankind and proves only that, since they are never satisfied with the present and have learned from experience to place little hope in the future, people adorn the irrevocable past with all the flowers of their imagination.

Here is what we know for certain. The village of Goriukhino has belonged since ancient times to the illustrious family of Belkin. But my ancestors, who owned many other estates, paid scant attention to this remote land. Goriukhino was lightly taxed and was administered by elders elected by the villagers at meetings known as peasant councils.

But with the passage of time the Belkins' family holdings fragmented and fell into decline. The impoverished grandsons of a wealthy grandfather were unable to give up their former luxurious ways and, from estates now shrunk to a tenth of their original size, they attempted to extract the same income as in years gone by. The village received threatening injunctions, one after another. The elder read them aloud to the council; venerable figures waxed eloquent, there was general agitation, and, instead of a double quitrent, the lords and masters of the village received only sly excuses and humble complaints written on greasy paper and sealed with a half-kopek coin.

A dark cloud hung over Goriukhino, but no one seemed even to notice it. And then, in the final year of the reign of Trifon—the last elder to be chosen by the village commune—on the feast day of the village's patron saint, when the entire population was either noisily crowding around the recreational establishment (in the vernacular—"the pothouse") or else wandering up and down the streets arm in arm, singing the songs of Arkhip the Bald at the top of their voices, a wicker-covered carriage drove into the village. It was drawn by a pair of half-dead nags. A ragged-looking Jew sat on the box, and a head in a peaked cap poked out of the window, peering at the merrymakers with what seemed like some interest. The villagers greeted the carriage with laughter and crude taunts. (N.B. Rolling the hems of their clothes into tubes, the fools mocked the Jewish coachman, calling out facetiously, "Jew, Jew, Jew, go chew on a pig's ear!"—chronicle of the Goriukhino sexton.) Imagine everyone's surprise when the carriage drew up in the middle of the village and the new arrival jumped out and imperiously demanded to speak to Trifon the village elder. This dignitary happened at that moment to be inside the recreational establishment. Two of the older peasants escorted him out, each supporting him by one arm. The stranger looked sternly at Trifon, handed him a letter, and ordered him to read it forthwith. But it was not the way of the elders of Goriukhino to read anything for themselves. Trifon could neither read nor write. Someone sent for Avdey the village clerk. He was located not far away, asleep under a fence in a side street, and brought before the stranger.

But either sudden fright or sad presentiment made the clearly traced letters appear blurred to him, and he was unable to decipher them. With terrible curses the stranger sent both Trifon the elder and Avdey the clerk off to bed, postponed the reading of the letter till the following day, and went to the steward's hut. The Jew followed him, carrying his small case.

The Goriukhinites watched these unusual proceedings in silent amazement, but the carriage, the Jew, and the stranger were soon forgotten. The day ended noisily and merrily, and Goriukhino fell asleep with no inkling of what lay in store for it.

At sunrise, the citizens were awakened by a knock on their windows and a summons to a village assembly. One by one, they appeared in the yard of the steward's hut, which served as a communal meeting place. Their eyes were red and bleary, and their cheeks puffy; yawning and scratching themselves, they looked at the man in the peaked cap and faded blue kaftan standing importantly on the porch of the steward's hut. No one was certain whether or not they had seen him before. Trifon the elder and Avdey the clerk stood close by; they had taken their hats off and were looking both servile and profoundly distressed.

"Is everybody here?" asked the stranger.

"Every one of you here?" repeated the elder.

"Yes," answered the citizens.

The elder then announced that a letter had come from their landlord, and he ordered the clerk to read it aloud for all to hear. Avdey stepped forward and, in a voice like thunder, read the sentences that follow. (N.B. The Goriukhino chronicler writes, "I copy this dread document at the home of Trifon elder where it be kept in the icon case in company of other memorials of his reign over Goriukhino." I myself was unable to trace this curious document.)

Trifon Ivanov,

The bearer of this letter, my representative ——, has been appointed to take over the management of my family estate, the village of Goriukhino. Forthwith upon his arrival you are to summon all the peasants and declare to them their master's will: namely, that they, the peasants, are to obey the commands of my representative —— as they would my own. And they shall comply absolutely in every respect, or he will respond with the utmost severity. What has compelled me to take this step, Trifon Ivanov, is their unconscionable disobedience, along with your own roguish connivance.

(signed) N. N.

With his feet wide apart and his hands on his hips, as if to form the letters X and Φ, ——[29] then came out with a brief but expressive speech: "So you'd better look out. You won't get away with any of your smart tricks now. I know you're a spoiled lot, but I'll knock any nonsense out of your heads quicker than you can say goodbye to your hangovers."

But everyone was already stone-cold sober. Aghast and hanging their heads, the Goriukhinites went back to their homes. It was indeed as if they had been struck by a bolt from the sky.

THE RULE OF THE STEWARD ——

—— took up the reins of government and set about implementing a political system that merits special analysis.

It was founded on the following axiom: the richer the peasant, the more troublesome; and conversely, the poorer, the humbler. And so —— set about promoting humility as the cardinal peasant virtue. He demanded an inventory of the peasant households and divided them into rich and poor.

1. The village's arrears of rent were apportioned among the rich peasants and exacted from them with the utmost severity.

2. Paupers and work-shy wastrels were immediately set to the plow, and if their work failed to measure up, the steward assigned them as laborers to other peasants, for which the latter paid him a voluntary tribute. Peasants delivered into bondage had the full right to redeem themselves by paying a double quitrent on top of their share of the arrears. All communal obligations fell on the shoulders of the more prosperous peasants. The avaricious steward's greatest triumph of all was the system of military conscription; one by one, the prosperous peasants bought themselves off, until there was no one left except

some scoundrel or ne'er-do-well.* Meetings of the village assembly were suspended. Quitrent was collected piecemeal, throughout the year. From time to time, there were unexpected supplementary levies. The peasants did not appear to be paying a great deal more than they had before, yet it was impossible for them ever to earn or save enough money. Within three years Goriukhino was destitute.

The village had become a wretched place; the market was deserted and the songs of Arkhip the Bald went unsung. Young children left their homes to go begging. Half of the peasants worked on the fields, while the other half were in bondage. The day of the village's patron saint was now, in the words of the chronicler, "not a day of joy and celebration, but an anniversary of sorrow and a commemoration of bitter grief."

Translated by Robert and Elizabeth Chandler

---

*The accursed steward put Anton Timofeyev in fetters till old Timofey ransomed his son for one hundred rubles. The steward clapped Petrushka Yeremeyev in irons till his father bought him for sixty-eight rubles. Next the damned one wanted to shackle Lekha Tarasov, but the latter ran off into the forest. Exceedingly vexed, the steward cursed and raged in wild words. In the end, Vanka the drunkard was taken away to town and delivered into conscription." (From the complaint lodged by the Goriukhino peasants.)

DUBROVSKY

PART ONE

I

SEVERAL years ago, on one of his estates, there lived a Russian gentleman of the old school, Kirila Petrovich Troyekurov. His wealth, connections, and distinguished lineage made him an important figure in the provinces where his estates were located. His neighbors were glad to indulge his slightest whims and local officials trembled when they heard his name. Kirila Petrovich accepted these signs of servility as his due; his house was always full of guests willing to share in his noisy, sometimes even riotous, pursuits and so help him while away his hours of gentlemanly leisure. No one dared turn down an invitation from him or ventured not to come to the village of Pokrovskoye, on certain days of the year, to pay his respects. In his domestic life Kirila Petrovich exhibited all the vices of a man without education. Spoiled by everything around him, he was accustomed to giving free rein to every impulse of his hot-blooded nature and every whim of his somewhat limited mind. Despite his unusually strong constitution, he suffered from the effects of gluttony about twice every week, and he was tipsy every evening. In one wing of his house he kept sixteen chambermaids—sewing, embroidering, and working at other ladylike tasks. The windows in this wing were protected by wooden bars; the doors were secured by locks whose keys he looked after himself. At appointed hours the young recluses, watched over by two old women, went out for walks in the garden. Now and again Kirila Petrovich would give some of them away in marriage, and new ones would take their place. His treatment of his peasants and house serfs was severe and willful; yet they were proud of their master's wealth and reputation, and they in turn took many liberties with their neighbors, trusting in his powerful protection.

Troyekurov invariably spent his days riding on horseback about his extensive estates, enjoying prolonged feasts, and playing pranks, new examples of which he invented daily and whose victim was usually some new acquaintance, although even old friends were not always exempt—with the single exception of Andrey Gavrilovich Dubrovsky. This Dubrovsky, a retired Guards lieutenant, was his closest neighbor, and the owner of seventy serfs. Troyekurov behaved arrogantly towards people of the very highest rank but always treated Dubrovsky with respect, in spite of the latter's humble standing. At one time they had served together, and Troyekurov remembered his former comrade's hot temper and resoluteness only too well. Circumstances, however, had separated them for many years. Dubrovsky, his estate in disorder, had no choice but to retire from the Guards and settle down in what remained of his village.[1] Kirila Petrovich, learning of this, had offered him assistance, but Dubrovsky had thanked him and remained poor and independent. Some years later, Troyekurov, by then a full general, also retired to his estate; they met again and were overjoyed to see one another. Since then, they had met every day, and Kirila Petrovich, who had never in his life graced anyone with a visit, would call at his friend's little house without the least ceremony. They were of the same age and had been born into the same social class and received the same education; they also had much in common with regard to character and general disposition. In some respects their fates had been similar: both had married for love, both had soon been widowed, and each had been left with a single child. Dubrovsky's son was being educated in Petersburg, while Troyekurov's daughter was being brought up at home; Troyekurov often used to say to Dubrovsky, "Listen, brother Andrey Gavrilovich, if your Volodka grows up with a head on his shoulders, he can marry my Masha. Never mind if he's as poor as a church mouse." Andrey Gavrilovich would shake his head and answer, "No, Kirila Petrovich. My Volodka's no husband for your Maria Kirilovna. A poor gentleman like him is better off marrying a poor gentlewoman—and being head of the household—than marrying a spoiled hussy and ending up as her steward."

Everyone envied the harmony between the arrogant Troyekurov and his poor neighbor, and everyone marveled at the latter's boldness when he spoke out straightforwardly at Kirila Petrovich's table, not worrying whether his opinions contradicted his host's. Some tried to imitate him, stepping beyond the boundaries of due subservience, but Kirila Petrovich gave them such a fright that none of them ever dared anything of the kind again, and Dubrovsky alone remained outside the general law. Everything, however, was turned upside down by an unexpected event.

Early one autumn, Kirila Petrovich was making preparations to go hunting. The day before the hunt, the grooms and kennel-men were ordered to be ready by five o'clock the following morning. A tent and a field kitchen were sent ahead to the place where Kirila Petrovich expected to dine. Meanwhile, the host and his guests went out to look at the kennels, where more than five hundred hounds and borzois lived in comfort and warmth, praising Kirila Petrovich's generosity in their canine tongue. There was not only a hospital for sick dogs, under the supervision of staff physician Timoshka, but also a section where noble bitches whelped and suckled their puppies. Kirila Petrovich was proud of this splendid establishment and never missed a chance to show it off to his guests, each of whom had already inspected it at least twenty times. Surrounded by his guests and accompanied by Timoshka and the chief kennel-men, Kirila Petrovich strolled slowly round; stopping outside particular kennels, he would ask questions about the health of sick dogs, make observations of varying degrees of justice and severity, or call out to dogs he knew and talk to them affectionately. The guests considered it their duty to express their admiration. Only Dubrovsky frowned and said nothing. He was a passionate hunter. His circumstances allowed him to keep only two hounds and one pack of borzois; he couldn't but feel a certain envy at the sight of this magnificent establishment. "Why are you frowning, Brother?" Kirila Petrovich asked him. "Do you not like my kennels?" "No," Dubrovsky answered sullenly, "your kennels are wonderful. I doubt if your servants live as well as your dogs." One of the kennel-men took exception to this. "Thanks be to God and to our master," he said, "we have no complaints, but in all truth there are gentlemen who'd be onto a good thing if they could exchange their estates for any one of these here kennels. They'd be warmer—and better fed." Kirila Petrovich laughed loudly at his serf's impudent remark, and his guests laughed too, even though each felt that the man's joke might have been directed at him in person. Dubrovsky went pale and said nothing. Just then some newborn puppies were brought to Kirila Petrovich in a basket, and for a while they took up his attention; he chose two to keep and ordered the rest to be drowned. In the meantime Dubrovsky disappeared, and no one noticed.

On returning from the kennels, Kirila Petrovich and his guests sat down to supper; only then did Kirila Petrovich realize that his friend was missing. He was told that Andrey Gavrilovich had returned home. He ordered someone to gallop after him and bring him back immediately. Never yet had Kirila Petrovich gone out hunting without Dubrovsky, who was an experienced and discriminating judge of canine merits and an unerring adjudicator of every possible kind of hunting dispute. The servant sent after Dubrovsky came back while they were still at table; he reported to his master that Andrey Gavrilovich had refused to listen and had not returned with him. Kirila Petrovich, in his usual state of tipsy excitability, was enraged. He sent the same servant back after Andrey Gavrilovich to insist that he return to Pokrovskoye at once and stay the night; otherwise, he, Troyekurov, would sever relations with him forever. The servant galloped off again. Kirila Petrovich got up from the table and, leaving his guests to find their way to their rooms, retired to bed.

His first question the following morning was "Is Andrey Gavrilovich here?" By way of an answer he was given a letter, folded into a triangle. Kirila Petrovich ordered his scribe to read it and heard the following:

Most gracious sir,

I do not intend to visit Pokrovskoye until you send me your huntsman Paramoshka with an admission of his guilt; whether I punish or pardon him will be at my pleasure, and I do not intend to endure jests from your serfs and I will not endure them from you, since I myself am no clown but a nobleman of ancient lineage. Meanwhile I remain at your disposal,[2]

Andrey Dubrovsky

By today's standards of etiquette, this letter would be considered most incorrect; Kirila Petrovich, however, was angered not by its strange style and composition but by its substance. "What!" he thundered, leaping out of bed in his bare feet. "I'm to send him my servants with admissions of guilt and it will be his pleasure to punish or pardon them! What's got into the man? Who does he take me for? I'll show him. He'll live to regret this—I'll teach him how to treat a Troyekurov!"

Kirila Petrovich dressed and rode out in his usual splendor, but the hunt was unsuccessful. They saw only one hare during the entire day, and it escaped. Dinner in the open fields under a tent was also unsuccessful, or at least not to the taste of Kirila Petrovich, who thrashed his cook and tongue-lashed his guests; on the way home, together with the whole hunt, he deliberately rode over Dubrovsky's fields.

Several days passed, and the enmity between the two neighbors did not abate. Dubrovsky did not go to Pokrovskoye. Without him, Kirila Petrovich felt bored and lonely, and his irritation poured out in the most abusive expressions which, thanks to the zeal of the local landowners, reached Dubrovsky with amendments and embellishments of every kind. Any last hope of reconciliation was destroyed by another incident.

Dubrovsky was riding round his small estate; nearing a birch copse, he heard the blows of an axe and, a minute later, the crash of a falling tree. He hurried into the copse and found peasants from Pokrovskoye, calmly stealing his timber. Seeing him, they tried to run off. Dubrovsky and his coachman caught two of them, bound them, and brought them back to the house. The victor's spoils also included three enemy horses. Dubrovsky was extremely angry: Troyekurov's men, known brigands, were aware of his friendship with their master and had never before dared get up to mischief on his property. Dubrovsky realized that they were taking advantage of the recent breach in relations, and he decided, contrary to all the conventions of war, to teach his prisoners a lesson, using the switches they had cut in his copse, and to put their three horses to work alongside his own.

Word of this event reached Kirila Petrovich that same day. In his first moments of fury he wanted to muster his house serfs, attack Kisteniovka[3] (as his neighbor's village was called), raze it to the ground, and besiege the landlord in his own house. To him, this would have been nothing unusual. But his thoughts were soon taken in a different direction.

Pacing heavy-footed up and down the hall, he happened to glance out of the window and see a troika stop by the gate; a small man in a leather cap and an overcoat of coarse frieze got out of the cart and went into a wing of the house to see the steward. Troyekurov recognized Shabashkin, the assessor, and sent for him. Within a minute Shabashkin was standing before Kirila Petrovich, bowing low bows and reverently awaiting his orders.

"Good day, Mr. whatever-your-name-is!" said Troyekurov. "What's brought you to us?"

"I was on my way to town, Your Excellency," said Shabashkin, "and I called in on Ivan Demyanov to see if Your Excellency had any orders."

"You've come just at the right time, Mr. whatever-your-name-is. I need you. Have some vodka and listen!"

The assessor was pleasantly amazed by this warm welcome. He refused the vodka and listened to Kirila Petrovich with all his attention.

"I have a neighbor," said Troyekurov, "a boor of a small landowner. I want to take his estate from him. What do you think?"

"Your Excellency, if you have some documents or—"

"Nonsense, my brother, what do we want with documents? What are court decrees for? How, I want you to tell me, without having any right to it, can I confiscate his estate? But wait a moment . . . The estate did once belong to us. We bought it from some fellow called Spitsyn, then sold it to Dubrovsky's father. Can't we make something of that?"

"It would be difficult, Your Highest Excellency. The sale was probably effected in a legal manner."

"Think, Brother. Rack your brains."

"If, for example, Your Excellency could somehow obtain from your neighbor the record or deed entitling him to his estate, then of course—"

"I understand—but the documents, unfortunately, were burnt during a fire."

"What, Your Excellency! The documents were burnt? What more could you ask for? In that case, you may proceed in accordance with the law, and I have no doubt that you will receive your complete satisfaction."

"You think so? Well then, take good care. I rely on your zeal, and you may be assured of my gratitude."

Shabashkin bowed almost to the ground, drove away, and set to work that very day—and two weeks later, thanks to his expeditiousness, Dubrovsky was asked by the authorities to provide them at once with an adequate explanation of how he had come to be in possession of the village of Kisteniovka.

Amazed by this unexpected request, Andrey Gavrilovich immediately wrote a rather rude reply, stating that the village of Kisteniovka had come to him on the death of his father, that he held it by right of inheritance, that none of this was any of Troyekurov's business, and that any other party's claim to the property was a slander and fraud.

The impression made by this letter on Shabashkin, the assessor, was an extremely agreeable one. He could see, firstly, that Dubrovsky knew little about legal matters, and secondly, that it would not be difficult to place someone so imprudent and hot-tempered in an extremely awkward position. After considering the assessor's requests more coolly, Andrey Gavrilovich understood the need to reply in more detail. He wrote a fairly businesslike document, but even this was to prove insufficient.

The matter dragged on. Convinced of the rightness of his case, Andrey Gavrilovich troubled himself very little about it; he had neither the wish nor the means to throw money about, and, although he had always been the first to joke about how easy it was to buy the consciences of bureaucrats, it never occurred to him that he might himself become a victim of fraud. Troyekurov, for his part, showed equally little concern about winning the case he had initiated. Shabashkin, however, busied himself on Troyekurov's behalf, acted in his name, intimidated and bribed judges, and interpreted every possible decree every which way.

In the event, on the ninth day of February 18—, Dubrovsky received from the town police a summons to appear before the —— District Judge in order to hear the latter's ruling on the matter of the estate disputed between him, Lieutenant Dubrovsky, and Captain General Troyekurov, and to sign in testimony of his satisfaction or dissatisfaction. Dubrovsky left for town that same day; on the way he was overtaken by Troyekurov. They exchanged haughty glances, and Dubrovsky noticed a malicious smile on his adversary's face.

2

On his arrival in town, Andrey Gavrilovich stopped at the house of a merchant he knew and stayed the night with him; the following morning he appeared at the District Court. No one paid any attention to him. Kirila Petrovich arrived just after him. The clerks rose to their feet and put their pens behind their ears. The members of the court met him with expressions of profound servility and pulled up an armchair for him out of respect for his rank, years, and portliness. He sat down close to the door, which was left open. Still standing, Andrey Gavrilovich leaned against the wall. A deep silence set in, and the secretary began to read out the court's judgment in a ringing voice. We quote this in full, believing everyone will be pleased to learn of one of the methods by which we in Russia can be deprived of an estate to which our rights are indisputable:

On the 27th day of October in the year 18— the —— District Court examined the case of the wrongful possession by Guards Lieutenant Andrey, son of Gavril, Dubrovsky, of an estate belonging to Captain General Kirila, son of Piotr, Troyekurov, and which comprises the village of Kisteniovka in the —— province, male serfs to the number of ——, and —— acres of land with meadows and all appurtenances. Concerning which matter it is evident that: on the 9th day of June in the past year of 18—, the said Captain General Troyekurov lodged a petition with this court, stating that, on the 14th day of August 17—, his late father, a Knight and Collegiate Assessor, Piotr, son of Yefim, Troyekurov, then serving with the rank of Provincial Secretary in the —— Vicegerent's Chancery,[4] did purchase from Chancery Clerk Fadey, son of Yegor, Spitsyn, of the nobility, the property comprising the aforesaid village of Kisteniovka (which village, at that time, according to the —— census, was known as the Kisteniov settlement), and, according to the —— census, male serfs to the number of ——, together with all their peasants' chattels, and also arable and nonarable land, forests, hay meadows, the fishing in the river known as the Kisteniovka, and all appurtenances of the above estate, together with a timber manorial house, and in short everything without remainder which came to him by inheritance from his father Sergeant Yegor, son of Terenty, Spitsyn, of the nobility, and which he held in his possession, not excepting a single serf or a single acre of land, for a price of 2,500 rubles, for which a deed of sale was registered on that same day in the chambers of the —— Court and Tribunal, and that his father, Collegiate Assessor Piotr, son of Yefim, Troyekurov on that 26th day of August took possession of this estate, this being registered in the District Court. And that lastly, on the 6th day of September in the year 17—, his father by the will of God passed away, while he himself, the aforesaid plaintiff Captain General Troyekurov had, almost since his infancy, from the year 17—, been serving in the army, and for most of that time had been campaigning in foreign lands, for which reason he was unable to receive intelligence either of his father's death or of the estate that had been left to him. Now, however, upon his final retirement from that service and his return to his father's estates, comprising, in the —— districts of the —— provinces, some several villages with 3,000 serfs in all, he discovers that one of these said villages with, according to the —— census, serfs to the number of —— (and according to the most recent census, serfs to the number of ——) is in the possession of the aforesaid Guards Lieutenant Andrey Dubrovsky, for which reason, presenting together with his petition the original deed of sale given to his father by the vendor, Spitsyn, he petitions that the aforesaid estate be removed from the wrongful possession of Dubrovsky and placed as it should be at his own full disposal. And with regard to the wrongful appropriation of the aforesaid estate, from which he has enjoyed revenues, he petitions that, after due investigation, lawful damages be exacted from Dubrovsky and satisfaction rendered to himself, Troyekurov.

"Investigations carried out by the —— District Court following upon this petition have revealed that: the aforesaid Guards Lieutenant Dubrovsky, currently in possession of the disputed estate, has deposed to the local Assessor of the Nobility that the estate currently in his possession, comprising the said village of Kisteniovka, together with serfs to the number of —— and all land and appurtenances thereto, came into his possession by inheritance, upon the death of his father, Second Lieutenant in the Artillery Gavril, son of Yevgraf, Dubrovsky, who himself purchased the estate from the father of the plaintiff, formerly Provincial Secretary and subsequently Collegiate Assessor Troyekurov, this being effected through a procuration granted on the 30th day of August in the year 17— and notarized in the —— District Court to Titular Councilor Grigory, son of Vasily, Sobolev, according to which there must have been drawn up a deed of purchase of this estate by his father, since the said procuration states that he, Troyekurov, had sold to Dubrovsky's father the entire estate, comprising serfs to the number of —— and land, and that he had received in full and not returned the 3,200 rubles due to him in accordance with their agreement, and that he had requested the aforementioned Sobolev to convey to him the said deed of purchase. This same procuration also stipulated that Dubrovsky's father, in consideration of his having paid the entire sum due, should take possession of the said estate and dispose of it as its rightful owner, even before the completion of the said deed of purchase, and that neither the vendor, Troyekurov, nor any other person should henceforth interfere with the property. But when exactly and at which office the aforesaid deed of purchase was given to his father by the attorney Sobolev, he, Andrey Dubrovsky, did not know, having been at that time still a minor, and because after his father's death he was unable to find said deed of purchase and he supposes said deed to have been destroyed, along with other documents and property, in a fire that occurred in their house in the year 17—, and which the inhabitants of said village remember well. And that, since the day of the sale by Troyekurov or of the issue of the procuration to Sobolev, that is since the year 17—, and following the death of his father in 17—, and up until the present day, the Dubrovskys have been in undisputed possession of this estate, to all of which the local inhabitants, fifty-two in number, have testified under oath that indeed, as they can well remember, the Dubrovskys first came into possession of the aforesaid estate seventy years previously, and without dispute, but by what deed or title they do not know. Whether the aforementioned prior purchaser of the estate, Piotr Troyekurov, formerly Provincial Secretary, enjoyed possession of this estate, they do not remember. The house in the possession of the Dubrovsky family did indeed burn down some thirty years ago, in a fire that took hold in the village at night; and it was generally reckoned that the annual revenue from the disputed estate, all in all, from that time until the present day, had amounted to no less than two thousand rubles.

In response, on the 3rd day of January of the present year, Captain General Kirila, son of Piotr, Troyekurov petitioned this court to find that although the aforesaid Guards Lieutenant Andrey Dubrovsky had, in the course of this present investigation, submitted as evidence the procuration given by his late father Gavril Dubrovsky to Titular Councilor Sobolev with regard to the purchase of said estate, he had not, through this document, provided, as required by Chapter Nineteen of the General Regulations and by the edict of 29 November 1752, any genuine deed of title, or indeed any clear evidence of the execution, at any time, of such a deed. Wherefore, this same procuration, after the death of its issuer, his father, is, according to the edict of the —— day of May 1818, entirely invalid.

Moreover, it has been decreed that the ownership of disputed estates shall be determined according to deed of title, if such a deed exists, and according to the results of an investigation, if such a deed proves not to exist.

Captain General Kirila, son of Piotr, Troyekurov has already submitted in evidence a deed of title to the said estate, formerly belonging to his father, and he therefore petitions, on the basis of the laws aforementioned, that the estate be removed from the possession of the aforesaid Dubrovsky and restored to himself as the rightful owner thereof by right of inheritance. And since the aforesaid landowners, having in their possession an estate to which they had no right or title, have wrongfully enjoyed revenues from this estate to which they have no entitlement, it should be established by law to what sum these said revenues amount and this sum should then be exacted from the landowner Dubrovsky and restored to him, Troyekurov, to his entire satisfaction.

Concerning the said disputed estate, now in the possession of Guards Lieutenant Andrey, son of Gavril, Dubrovsky, and which comprises the village of Kisteniovka and, according to the most recent census, male serfs to the number of ——, together with land and appurtenances, it is evident that Captain General Kirila, son of Piotr, Troyekurov, has submitted a valid deed of purchase of the same, in the year 17—, from Chancery Clerk Fadey, son of Yegor, Spitsyn, of the nobility, by his own late father, formerly Provincial Secretary and afterwards Collegiate Assessor. Furthermore, the said purchaser of the estate, Troyekurov, as appears from this title deed, was indeed that same year placed in possession of said estate by the —— District Court, with livery of seizin executed. And although Guards Lieutenant Dubrovsky has submitted in evidence a procuration given by the aforementioned deceased purchaser Troyekurov to Titular Councilor Sobolev for the completion of a deed of purchase by his father Dubrovsky, it is nevertheless expressly forbidden by Statute —— not only to confirm ownership of immovable real estate on such basis but even to enter into provisional ownership thereof; and moreover, the said procuration is itself rendered null and void by the death of its issuer. Furthermore, from the commencement of the present inquiry, that is, from the year 18—, and until the present day, no clear evidence has been submitted by Dubrovsky that any title deed in respect of the purchase of the said disputed estate was ever at any time or place completed. This Court therefore decrees: that the said estate, with serfs to the number of ——, with land and appurtenances, in whatsoever condition it should now be, be confirmed, in accordance with the title deed he has himself presented, as the property of Captain General Troyekurov; that Guards Lieutenant Dubrovsky be removed from the possession of said estate; and that seizin be granted to Troyekurov as by right of inheritance and that this be registered at the —— District Court. And that, although Captain General Troyekurov has furthermore petitioned for the exaction from Guards

Lieutenant Dubrovsky of the revenues enjoyed by him as a result of his wrongful possession of said estate, nevertheless, since the said estate, according to the testimony of inhabitants of long standing, has been in the undisputed possession of the Dubrovsky family for some years, and since there is no evidence that Mr. Troyekurov has ever before, regarding the Dubrovskys' wrongful possession of the said estate, lodged any petition on the basis of the decree that should one man sow the land of another or fence round his property, and should a petition be made regarding this unlawful seizure of land, and should an inquiry be held, then the said land shall be returned to the rightful owner thereof, together with the crops sewn, and the fencing, and any buildings.

For the reasons stated above, Captain General Troyekurov is to be denied the damages he has requested from Lieutenant Dubrovsky, since the estate belonging to him is being restored to his possession, without remainder. And the said estate is to be returned to him in its entirety, no part to be excepted, and should Captain General Troyekurov have any clear and legitimate grounds of complaint in this regard, he may therefore lodge a further petition at the appropriate court. This ruling is to be notified in advance to both plaintiff and defendant, together with its foundation in law and procedures for any appeal, plaintiff and defendant to be summoned by the police to this court that they may hear the ruling of the Court and sign in indication of their satisfaction or dissatisfaction.

The secretary finished; the assessor rose and, with a low bow, turned to Troyekurov, offering him the document to sign. The triumphant Troyekurov took the pen from him and signed the Court's decision, indicating his entire satisfaction.

It was then Dubrovsky's turn. The secretary handed him the document. But Dubrovsky remained motionless, head bowed.

The secretary repeated his invitation to sign, asking Dubrovsky to indicate his complete and entire satisfaction, or his manifest dissatisfaction if, contrary to expectation, feeling in all conscience that his case was just, he intended to appeal within the legally appointed time to the appropriate court. Dubrovsky said nothing. Suddenly he raised his head. His eyes flashed. He stamped his foot, pushed the secretary out of the way so forcefully that he fell to the ground, then seized the inkwell and flung it at the assessor. Everyone was appalled.

"What!" Dubrovsky yelled out. "Have you no respect for the church of the Lord? Out of my way, churls!" Turning to Kirila Petrovich, he continued, "It's unheard of, Your Excellency! Kennel-men bringing their dogs into the church of the Lord! Dogs running about the church! I'll teach you!"

Hearing the uproar, the guards rushed in and only with difficulty managed to overpower Dubrovsky. He was led out and put onto his sledge.

Troyekurov went out after him, accompanied by the entire court. Dubrovsky's crazed outburst had made a powerful impression on him and poisoned his triumph.

The judges, who had counted on his gratitude, were not honored with so much as a single friendly word. Troyekurov went straight back to Pokrovskoye. Dubrovsky, meanwhile, lay in bed; the district physician, fortunately not a complete ignoramus, successfully bled him and applied leeches and Spanish fly.[5] Towards evening the sick man began to feel better, and he recovered his senses. The following day he was taken to Kisteniovka, though this now barely belonged to him.

3

Some time had gone by, but poor Dubrovsky was still not well. True, there were no more fits of madness, but his strength was visibly failing. He forgot his former occupations, rarely left his room, and was lost in thought for days on end. He was now being nursed by Yegorovna, a kindhearted old woman who had at one time looked after his son. She cared for him as if he were a child, reminded him when it was time to eat or sleep, fed him, and put him to bed. Andrey Gavrilovich quietly obeyed her and had no contact with anyone else. He was in no state to think about his affairs or take care of his property, and Yegorovna decided she must inform his son, who was then in St. Petersburg, serving in one of the regiments of the Foot Guards. And so, tearing out a page from the household accounts book, she dictated a letter to Khariton the cook, the only person in Kisteniovka who could read and write, and sent it off to the town to be posted.

But it is time we acquainted the reader with the real hero of our story.

Vladimir Dubrovsky had been educated at the military academy and then joined the Horse Guards with the rank of cornet;[6] his father spared nothing to support him in style, and the young man received more money from home than he had any right to expect. Prodigal and ambitious, he indulged himself in extravagant whims, played cards and ran up debts, careless about the future and imagining that sooner or later he would find himself a rich bride—the usual dream of poor young men.

One evening, as several officers sat in his rooms, sprawling on his sofas and smoking his pipes, which had amber mouthpieces, his valet Grisha handed him a letter. He was immediately struck by the seal and handwriting. He quickly broke the seal and read,

Our dear Master Vladimir Andreyevich,

I, your old nyanya, have resolved to inform you of your Papa's health. He is very poorly, sometimes he wanders in his talk, and he sits there all day like a foolish child—but life and death are in the hands of the Lord. Come home to us soon, light of my eyes, we'll send the horses out to Pesochnoye for you. We have heard the District Court are coming to hand us over to Kirila Petrovich Troyekurov, since they say we belong to him, but we have belonged to your family forever and I have never heard such a thing since the day I was born. You could, living in Petersburg, report this to our father the Tsar, and he won't let us be wronged. I remain your faithful slave and nurse,
Orina Yegorovna Byzyreva

I send my mother's blessing to Grisha, is he serving you well? It's been raining for over a week now and Rodya the shepherd died close to St. Micholas's day.[7]

Vladimir Dubrovsky read these somewhat confused lines several times with unusual agitation. He had lost his mother in early childhood and been sent to Petersburg in his eighth year, barely knowing his father; nevertheless, he felt a romantic attachment to him and he loved family life all the more for never having had the opportunity to experience its quiet joys.

The thought of losing his father greatly pained his heart, and the condition of this poor sick man, which he surmised from his nurse's letter, filled him with horror. He imagined his father abandoned in a remote village, in the care of a stupid old woman and a few house serfs, threatened by some disaster and fading away, with no one to help him, in torment of body and soul. Vladimir reproached himself for his criminal neglect. It was a long time since he had received any letters from his father and he had not thought of making any inquiries, supposing his father either to be traveling somewhere or to be engrossed in the management of his estate.

He resolved to go and visit him, and even to retire from service should his father's condition require his continued presence. Seeing his anxiety, his comrades went on their way. Vladimir then wrote an application for leave of absence, lit a pipe, and sank into deep thought.

He handed in his application later that evening; and three days later he was on the highway.

Vladimir Andreyevich was nearing the post station where he would be turning off for Kisteniovka. His heart was full of sad forebodings; he was afraid of finding his father no longer alive; he was imagining the dismal life awaiting him in the country: a godforsaken village, loneliness, poverty, and struggles to sort out affairs of which he understood nothing. On reaching the post station, he went into the office and asked if there were private horses for hire. After inquiring where he was going, the postmaster said that horses from Kisteniovka had been waiting for him for over three days. Very soon old Anton the coachman appeared; in the past he had allowed Vladimir to go round the stable with him and had looked after his little pony. At the sight of Vladimir, Anton burst into tears, made a deep bow, said that the old master was still alive, and rushed off to harness the horses. Eager to set off, Vladimir refused the meal that was offered to him. Anton drove him along the little country lanes, and the two of them began to talk.

"Please tell me, Anton, what's this I hear about my father and Troyekurov?"

"Heaven knows, Master Vladimir Andreyevich...Your father, they say, fell foul of Kirila Petrovich, who took him to court, though often enough Kirila Petrovich is his own judge and jury. It's not for us serfs to question our masters, but your father didn't ought to have taken on Kirila Petrovich: you can't break an axe with a whip."

"So this Kirila Petrovich seems to do as he pleases round here?"

"That's the truth, master. He doesn't give a cuss for the assessor, and the police captain's at his beck and call. The gentry gather at his house and they dance attendance on him. As the saying goes: 'Set down a trough—and the pigs will come.'"

"Is it true he's taking away our estate?"

"Ay, master, that's what we hear tell. Just the other day the sexton from Pokrovskoye says at a christening in our elder's house, 'Your good times have come to an end now. Kirila Petrovich will take you in hand good and proper.' And Mikita the blacksmith, he answers him, 'Enough of that, Savelich, don't go grieving the host and upsetting the guests. Kirila Petrovich is one master, and Andrey Gavrilovich is another master, and every one of us is in the hands of God and the Tsar.' But you can't sew buttons on others' mouths."

"So you don't want to be handed over to Troyekurov?"

"Be handed over to Kirila Petrovich! Lord save and preserve us all! His own people often fare badly enough. If he gets his hands on strangers, he'll do worse than skin 'em—he'll tear off their flesh. No,

God grant long life to Andrey Gavrilovich, and should the Lord take him away from us, we none of us want no master but you, our benefactor. You stand by us, and we'll stand by you!"

Touched by the old coachman's devotion, Dubrovsky fell silent and once again gave himself up to his thoughts. Over an hour went by; he was roused by an exclamation from his valet, Grisha: "Look— Pokrovskoye!" Dubrovsky looked up. He was on the shore of a broad lake; from it flowed a small river that then wound its way between hills: on one of these hills, above the thick green of trees, could be seen a green roof and the belvedere of a huge stone house; on another hill stood a five-domed church and an old bell tower; scattered round about were peasant huts with their wells and vegetable plots. Dubrovsky recognized all this. He remembered how he had played on that first hill with little Masha Troyekurova, two years his junior, and promising, even then, to be a beauty. He wanted to ask Anton about her, but some kind of shyness held him back.

As they drew close to the manor house, he caught a glimpse of a white dress between the trees of the orchard. Just then Anton whipped on the horses and, impelled by the pride common to both country coachmen and city cabbies, rushed full tilt over the bridge and through the village. Leaving the village, they climbed a hill and Vladimir caught sight of a birch wood and, on some open ground to the left, a little gray house with a red roof. His heart beat faster. Before him he could see Kisteniovka and his father's sad home.

Ten minutes later he was driving into the courtyard. He looked about him with indescribable emotion. It was twelve years since he had seen his birthplace. What had then been little birch saplings, newly planted beside the fence, had grown into tall spreading trees. The courtyard itself, once graced with three neat flowerbeds separated by broad, carefully swept paths, was now an unmowed meadow where a hobbled horse was grazing. The dogs began to bark, but, recognizing Anton, they fell silent and wagged their shaggy tails. The house serfs all spilled out of their huts and surrounded the young master with loud exclamations of joy. With difficulty he squeezed through the eager crowd and reached the dilapidated steps; Yegorovna met him in the entrance room. "Greetings, my dear old nurse! Greetings!" he repeated, pressing the kind old woman to his heart. "And what about Papa? Where's Papa? How is he?"

At that moment, barely able to drag one foot after the other, a tall, thin man came into the room; he looked pale and old, and was wearing a gown and a nightcap.

"Greetings, Volodka!" he said in a weak voice, and Vladimir passionately embraced his father. The invalid's joy was too great a shock for him; he grew faint, his legs gave way beneath him, and but for his son's support he would have collapsed.

"Why did you get out of bed?" said Yegorovna. "You can barely stand—but you still want to join every gathering!"

The sick man was carried back to his bedroom. He tried to talk to his son, but the thoughts were confused and his speech disconnected. He fell silent and dozed off. Vladimir was shaken by his father's condition. He installed himself in his father's bedroom and asked to be left alone with him. The servants obeyed and all turned their attentions to Grisha, leading him to the servants' hall, where they welcomed him with the utmost cordiality, feasted him village-style, and exhausted him with questions and greetings.

4

Where once was festive fare, now stands a coffin.[8]

A few days after his arrival, young Dubrovsky wanted to take up the matter of the estate, but his father was in no condition to provide the necessary explanations; nor was there an attorney. Going through his father's papers, Vladimir found only the assessor's letter and a draft reply; this was not enough to give him any clear understanding of the lawsuit, and he made up his mind to await developments, trusting to the justness of his family's cause.

In the meantime Andrey Gavrilovich's health was worsening by the hour. Vladimir saw that the end was near and never left his side; the old man had now fallen into a state of complete infancy.

Meanwhile the appointed day came and went, and no appeal had been lodged. Kisteniovka now belonged to Troyekurov. Shabashkin appeared, bowing, congratulating Troyekurov, and asking when His High Excellency wished to take possession of his newly acquired property and whether His High Excellency preferred to do this in person or to commission a representative. Kirila Petrovich felt confused. He was not avaricious by nature; his desire for revenge had led him too far; his conscience was murmuring. He knew about the present condition of his adversary, the old comrade of his youth, and victory brought no joy to his heart. He glared at Shabashkin, searching for some reason to give him a good cursing. Finding no adequate pretext, he said angrily, "Not you again. Go away."

Shabashkin, seeing Troyekurov was in a bad mood, bowed and hurried off. Left on his own, Kirila Petrovich began to pace up and down the room, whistling, "Thunder of Victory, Resound!"[9] always a sign that he was unusually agitated.

In the end he ordered his racing droshky[10] to be harnessed, put on a warm coat (it was the end of September), and drove out, taking the reins himself.

Soon he could see Andrey Gavrilovich's little house, and his soul was filled with contradictory emotions. Love of power and the satisfaction of vengeance had to some degree stifled his nobler feelings, but the latter finally gained the upper hand. He resolved to make peace with his old neighbor, and to destroy all traces of the quarrel by restoring the property to him. His soul eased by these good intentions, Kirila Petrovich approached his neighbor's house at a trot and drove straight into the courtyard.

The sick man was sitting at his bedroom window. He recognized Kirila Petrovich and a look of terrible confusion appeared on his face: a purple flush took the place of his usual pallor, his eyes flashed, he uttered unintelligible sounds. Young Dubrovsky, sitting over the household accounts, looked up and felt alarm at the change in his father. The sick man was pointing into the yard with a look of horror and rage. He was hurriedly gathering the folds of his dressing gown, meaning to get up from his chair; he half rose to his feet—and fell. His son rushed over to him; the old man was unconscious and not breathing; he had had a stroke. "Quick, quick, send for the doctor! Send someone into town!" Vladimir shouted. "Kirila Petrovich would like to see you," said a servant in the doorway. Vladimir gave him a terrible look.

"Tell Kirila Petrovich to leave here at once, before I have him thrown out . . . Now!" The servant delightedly rushed from the room to carry out his master's command. Yegorovna threw up her hands. "Dearest master," she squealed, "you're bringing ruin down onto your own head! Kirila Petrovich will devour us." "Be quiet, nurse," said Vladimir angrily. "Send Anton off for a doctor at once." Yegorovna left the room.

There was no one at all in the front hall; the servants had all run out to look at Kirila Petrovich. Yegorovna went out onto the porch and heard the servant delivering the young master's answer. Still sitting in his droshky, Kirila Petrovich heard him out. His face went darker than night; he smiled contemptuously, looked threateningly at the servants, and drove slowly round the yard. He glanced at the window where Andrey Gavrilovich had been sitting a minute before, but he was no longer there. The old nurse was standing on the porch, forgetting her master's orders. The servants were all holding forth. Suddenly Vladimir appeared and said, "There's no need for a doctor. Father has died."

There was confusion. The servants rushed into their old master's room. He was lying in the armchair where Vladimir had carried him; his right hand hung down to the floor, his head lolled on his chest; there was no sign of life in a body still warm but already disfigured by death. Yegorovna let out a wail. The servants surrounded the corpse now left to their care. They washed it, dressed it in a uniform sewn for Andrey Gavrilovich in 1797, and laid it out upon the table their master had sat at for so many years while they waited upon him.

5

The funeral took place on the third day. The poor old man's body lay on the table, covered by a shroud and surrounded by candles. The dining room was full of house serfs. The preparations had been completed.

Vladimir and three servants lifted the coffin. The priest walked in front; the sexton was at his side, singing the burial prayers. The master of Kisteniovka crossed the threshold of his house for the last time. The coffin was carried through the birch wood; the church lay just beyond it. It was a clear, cold day. Autumn leaves were falling from the trees.

As they left the wood, they saw Kisteniovka's wooden church and the graveyard, shaded by old lindens. There lay the body of Vladimir's mother; a fresh pit had been dug next to her grave the evening before.

The church was full of Kisteniovka peasants come to pay their last respects to their master. Young Dubrovsky stood by the choir; he neither wept nor prayed, but his face was terrifying. The sad rite came to an end. Vladimir went first to say goodbye to the body; he was followed by all the house serfs. The lid was brought in and the coffin nailed shut. The women wailed loudly; the men occasionally wiped away tears with their fists. Vladimir and the same three peasants, accompanied by the entire village, carried the coffin to the cemetery. The coffin was lowered into the grave and everyone present threw a handful of sand over it. The pit was filled in; everyone bowed to the grave, then went on their way. Vladimir left quickly, before everyone else, and disappeared into the Kisteniovka wood.

Yegorovna, in his name, invited the priest and the rest of the clergy to the funeral dinner, saying that the young master himself would not be present—and so Father Anton, his wife Fedotovna, and the sexton set off for the manor house, talking with Yegorovna about the virtues of the deceased and the future that, most likely, awaited his heir. Troyekurov's visit, and the reception given to him, were already known to the entire neighborhood, and local know-alls were predicting serious consequences.

"What will be, will be," said the priest's wife, "but I'll be sorry if Vladimir Andreyevich isn't to be our landlord. He's a fine fellow, there's no denying it."

"Who but he can ever be our landlord?" Yegorovna interjected. "It's in vain Kirila Petrovich gets himself so fired up—my young falcon's not so easily scared. He can stand up for himself, yes, and, God willing, his protectors won't abandon him either. And Kirila Petrovich may think himself ever so high and mighty, but he went off with his tail between his legs all right when my Grishka shouted: 'Be off, you old cur! Out of the yard with you!' "

"Mercy on us, Yegorovna!" said the sexton. "I'm surprised Grigory's tongue didn't refuse to obey him. For my part, I'd sooner lay complaints against the bishop himself than look disrespectfully at Kirila Petrovich. The moment I see him, I'm all bowed down with fear and trembling, and my back just bends and bends and goes on bending."

"Vanity of vanities," said the priest. "One day 'Eternal Memory' will be sung over Kirila Petrovich just as it was sung over Andrey Gavrilovich today. The funeral may be a little grander, and there may be more guests invited back afterwards, but it's all one and the same to God!"

"Oh father! We wanted to invite the whole neighborhood, but Vladimir Andreyevich refused. We've surely got enough of everything, we wouldn't be put to shame, but what could I do? Well, at least I've put out a nice spread for you, dear guests."

This cordial invitation and the hope of finding a tasty pie quickened the guests' steps. They soon arrived back at the house, where the table was already laid and the vodka waiting.

Meanwhile Vladimir was deep in the wood, attempting to tire himself out and stifle his sorrow. He walked without thinking where he was going; he kept being caught and scratched by branches, his feet sank into the bog, but he noticed nothing. After some time he reached a little hollow, surrounded by forest; a stream wound its way silently beside trees half stripped by autumn. Vladimir stopped; he sat down on the cold turf; thoughts crowded his mind, each gloomier than the one before. He was overwhelmed by loneliness. Storm clouds hung over his future. The feud with Troyekurov held out the promise of new misfortunes. His modest property might be taken away from him, which would leave him destitute. For a long time he sat in one spot without moving, watching the stream's quiet flow carrying away a few withered leaves—an image of life as true as it was commonplace. Eventually he realized it was growing dark; he got to his feet and began to look for the way home, but he had to wander a long time through the unfamiliar wood before he stumbled on the path that led to the gates of his house.

Coming straight towards him were the priest and his party. This was a bad omen, he thought immediately.[11] He involuntarily turned aside and hid behind a tree. No one noticed him, and they carried on talking heatedly as they passed by.

"Depart from evil, and do good,"[12] the priest was saying to his wife. "There's no need for us to hang about. However it ends, it's not you who's in trouble." Vladimir was unable to hear the wife's answer.

As he drew near his house, he saw a large number of people; both peasants and house serfs had crowded into the yard. Even from a distance Vladimir could hear an unusual hubbub. There were two troikas beside the barn. On the porch were several men he didn't know, wearing official uniforms and apparently discussing something.

"What's all this?" he asked angrily as Anton ran forwards to meet him. "Who are these men? What do they want?"

"Oh, my dear master," the old man answered with a sigh. "It's officers from the court. They're handing us over to Troyekurov, Vladimir Andreyevich, they're taking us away from Your Honor!"

Vladimir bowed his head; his serfs surrounded their luckless master. "You're our father," they shouted, kissing his hands. "We don't want no master but you. Just you give the word, sir—we can take care of these here officers. It may be our ruin, but we won't never betray you." Vladimir looked at them, stirred by unfamiliar feelings. "Stay where you are," he said, "while I speak to the officers." "That's right, master, you do that," shouted voices from the crowd. "Put the accursed wretches to shame! Have they no conscience?"

Vladimir went up to the officials. Shabashkin, cap on head, stood there with his arms akimbo, looking arrogantly around him. The police captain, a tall, stout man of about fifty, with a red face and a moustache, cleared his throat as he saw Dubrovsky coming towards him and pronounced in a hoarse voice: "And so I repeat what I have already said: by decree of the District Court you now all belong to Kirila Petrovich Troyekurov, whose person is here represented by Mr. Shabashkin. Obey him in all his commands; and you, women, must love and honor him, since he has a great love of you." The police captain burst out laughing at his witticism, and Shabashkin and the other officials followed his example. Vladimir was seething with indignation. "Allow me," he said with assumed calm, "to ask what all this means." "What this means," said the witty police captain, "is that we have come to place Kirila Petrovich Troyekurov in possession of this estate and to ask certain others to make themselves scarce while the going's good." "But you might, I think, have spoken to me before addressing my peasants, and let a landowner be the first to know that his estate no longer belongs to him—" "And who might you be?" Shabashkin asked with an insolent look. "The former land-owner, Andrey, son of Gavrila, Dubrovsky, has, by the will of God, passed away. As for you, we neither know you nor wish to know you."

"Vladimir Andreyevich is our young master," said a voice from the crowd.

"Who was that? Who dared to open his mouth?" asked the police captain menacingly. "Young master? Vladimir Andreyevich? Your master is Kirila Petrovich Troyekurov. Got that, blockheads?"

"Not on your life!" said the same voice.

"This is mutiny!" shouted the police captain. "Hey, where's the village elder?"

The village elder stepped forwards.

"Find me that man who spoke just then. I'll teach him!"

The elder turned to the crowd and asked who had spoken. But they all remained silent. After a while there were murmurs from the back of the crowd; these grew louder and quickly turned into the most terrible yells. The police captain then softened his voice and tried to calm them down. "Why are we just gaping at him?" shouted the house serfs. "Come on, lads, let's send 'em packing!" And the crowd surged forward. Shabashkin and the other officials rushed into the entrance room and locked the door behind them.

"Come on, let's tie 'em up!" shouted the same voice. And the crowd began to push against the door. "Stop!" shouted Dubrovsky. "What are you doing? You'll destroy both yourselves and me. Go back to your homes and leave me in peace. Don't be afraid—the tsar is merciful and I will appeal to him. He won't let us be wronged. We are all his children. But how can the tsar intercede on your behalf if you riot and carry on like brigands?"

Young Dubrovsky's words, and his resonant voice and commanding air, produced the desired effect. The crowd quietened down and dispersed; the yard emptied. The officials remained in the entrance room. Finally Shabashkin quietly opened the door, went out onto the porch, and, with obsequious bows, began to thank Dubrovsky for his merciful intervention. Vladimir listened to him with contempt and did not answer. "We have decided," the assessor continued, "to remain here, with your permission, for the night. It's dark already, and your peasants might attack us on the road. May I ask you to be so kind as to have some hay spread on the drawing-room floor for us to sleep on? At daybreak, we'll be on our way."

"Do as you please," Dubrovsky replied coldly. "I am no longer master here." With these words he withdrew into his father's room and locked the door behind him.

6

"So, it's the end of everything," Vladimir said to himself. "This morning I had a roof over my head and a crust of bread to eat. Tomorrow I shall be leaving the house where I was born and where my father died, leaving it to the man who killed my father and made a beggar of me." His eyes came to rest on a portrait of his mother. The painter had depicted her leaning against a balustrade, in a white morning dress and with a red rose in her hair. "And this portrait too will belong to the enemy of my family," he said to himself. "It'll be thrown into a lumber room along with some broken chairs, or else it'll be hung in his front hall, to be joked about by his kennel-men—and what was once her bedroom, this room where my father just died, will be given over to his steward, or to his harem. No! No! This sad house, from which I am being driven out, shall not belong to Troyekurov either." Vladimir clenched his teeth; terrible thoughts arose in his mind. He could hear the officials: they were lording it up, demanding now this, now that. Their voices were an unwelcome distraction from his sad thoughts. At last, everything fell silent.

Vladimir unlocked chests and drawers and began to go through his late father's papers. For the main part, they consisted of household accounts and business correspondence. Vladimir tore these up without reading them. Among them was a packet with the inscription "Letters from My Wife." With deep emotion, Vladimir began reading: the letters had been written at the time of the Turkish campaign[13] and sent to the army from Kisteniovka. His mother described her lonely life in the country and her management of the household; she tenderly lamented their long separation and begged her husband to come home to the embraces of a loving wife. In one letter she expressed anxiety about the health of little Vladimir; in another she rejoiced in his quick development and predicted a brilliant and happy future for him. His soul immersed in a world of family happiness, Vladimir forgot everything else, and he did not notice the passing of time. The wall clock struck eleven. Vladimir put the letters in his pocket, took a candle, and left the room. The officials were asleep on the floor of the drawing room. On the table stood the glasses they had emptied, and the room stank of rum. With a feeling of disgust, Vladimir walked past them into the front hall. The door to the entrance room was locked. Not finding the key, he returned to the drawing room; the key was on the table. Vladimir opened the door and bumped into a man crouching in a corner. An axe gleamed in his hand. Holding the candle towards him, Vladimir recognized Arkhip the blacksmith. "What are you doing here?" he asked. "Oh, Vladimir Andreyevich! It's you!" Arkhip whispered back. "Lord have mercy and save us! It's a good thing you were carrying a candle!" Vladimir looked at him in amazement. "What is it?" he asked the blacksmith. "What are you doing in here?"

"I wanted . . . I came . . . t-t-to see if the house was still . . ." Arkhip replied in a quiet stammer.

"And why the axe?"

"The axe? How can I go about at a time like this without an axe? These officials, you know, are scoundrels—you never can tell—"

"You're drunk. Put the axe down, and go and sleep it off."

"Drunk? Vladimir Andreyevich, dear master, God is my witness that not a drop has passed my lips. How could a man think of vodka at a time like this? Whoever heard of such a thing? Scribblers trying to take possession of us, driving our masters off their own property! Listen to them snoring, the accursed wretches! I could do away with the lot of them, and no one the wiser."

Dubrovsky frowned. "Listen, Arkhip," he said after a brief silence. "You must put thoughts like that out of your head. It's not the officials who are to blame. Just light your lantern and follow me."

Arkhip took the candle from his master's hand, found a lantern behind the stove, and lit it; the two of them went quietly down the steps and along one side of the yard. Someone on watch began to beat an iron plate; dogs barked. "Who's that?" asked Dubrovsky. "It's us, young master," answered a thin voice, "Vasilisa and Lukerya." "Go back home," said Dubrovsky, "We don't need you here." "Have a rest," added Arkhip. "Thank you, kind provider," said the women, and went straight back home.

Dubrovsky walked on. Two men approached; they called out to him. Dubrovsky recognized the voices of Anton and Grisha. "Why aren't you asleep?" he asked. "How can we sleep?" replied Anton. "Who'd have thought it—that we'd live to see—?"

"Quiet!" Dubrovsky interrupted. "Where's Yegorovna?"

"In the main house, in her little attic."

"Go and fetch her, and get all our people out of the house. See there's not a soul left indoors except the officials. And you, Anton, get a cart ready."

Grisha went off and reappeared a minute later with his mother. The old woman had not undressed; other than the officials, no one in the house had slept a wink.

"Is everyone here?" asked Dubrovsky. "No one left inside?"

"No one except the scribblers," said Grisha.

"Bring some hay or straw," said Dubrovsky.

The men ran to the stables and returned with armfuls of hay.

"Put it under the porch. And now, lads, a light!"

Arkhip opened up the lantern. Dubrovsky lit a splinter of wood.

"Wait a moment," he said to Arkhip. "I was in such a hurry I think I locked the door into the front hall. Go and unlock it."

Arkhip ran in. The door was unlocked. Arkhip locked it, muttering under his breath, "Unlock it? Not on your life!"—and returned to Dubrovsky.

Dubrovsky put the burning splinter to the hay. The hay caught fire. Flames leaped up, illuminating the courtyard.

"Mercy on us!" wailed Yegorovna. "Vladimir Andreyevich, what are you doing?"

"Quiet!" said Dubrovsky. "Farewell now, my children. I shall go where God leads me. Be happy with your new master."

"Father and provider," they all answered, "we're coming with you. We'd rather die than leave you."

The horses were led up. Dubrovsky climbed into the cart, along with Grisha, and told the others to meet him in the Kisteniovka wood. Anton struck the horses with his whip, and they drove out of the yard.

A wind got up. In a minute the whole house was in flames. Red smoke curled above the roof. Windowpanes cracked and fell out; burning beams began to collapse; there were pitiful wails and screams: "Help, we're burning! Help!" "Not on your life," said Arkhip, eyeing the blaze with a malicious smile. "Arkhipushka," Yegorovna said to him, "save the accursed wretches. God will reward you!'

"Not on your life," said the blacksmith.

The officials appeared at the windows, trying to smash the double frames. But then the roof crashed down and the screams ceased.

Soon all the domestic serfs were out in the yard. Shouting women were hurrying to save their few possessions; children jumped up and down, admiring the blaze. Sparks flew in a fiery whirlwind; the peasants' huts too were now catching fire.

"All as it should be," said Arkhip. "Burning well, isn't it? A fine sight from Pokrovskoye, I shouldn't wonder."

Just then something new attracted his attention: a cat was running about on the roof of the blazing barn, not knowing where to jump; it was surrounded by flame. The poor creature was mewing plaintively for help. Little boys were splitting their sides with laughter as they watched its despair. "Why are you laughing, you little devils?" said the blacksmith angrily. "Have you no fear of the Lord? One of God's creatures is dying, and you blockheads rejoice." He placed a ladder against the burning roof and climbed up. The cat understood what he was doing and, with a look of eager gratitude, clutched at his sleeve. Somewhat charred, the blacksmith climbed down with his catch. "Farewell now, good people," he said to the bewildered servants. "There's nothing left for me here. Good luck to you all. Remember me, don't think ill of me."

The blacksmith went off; the fire raged for some time. Finally it died down, though heaps of embers still glowed bright in the dark; around them wandered Kisteniovka's inhabitants, who had lost their all in the blaze.

7

The following day news of the fire spread round the entire neighborhood. Everyone offered their guesses and hypotheses. Some made out that Dubrovsky's servants, having got drunk at the funeral, had set fire to the house by mistake; others blamed the officials, saying it was they who had drunk too much while celebrating taking possession; many maintained that Dubrovsky himself had perished in the fire, along with the court officials and all the servants. Some guessed the truth and asserted that Dubrovsky himself, moved by fury and despair, was to blame for this terrible calamity. Troyekurov came round straightaway and personally conducted an investigation. It was established that the police captain and the assessor, the scrivener and the clerk of the District Court were all missing, in addition to Vladimir Dubrovsky himself, Yegorovna the old nurse, Anton the coachman, Arkhip the blacksmith, and the house serf Grigory. The house serfs all testified that the officials had been burned to death when the roof fell in; their charred bones were indeed discovered. The servant women Vasilisa and Lukerya said they had seen Dubrovsky and Arkhip the blacksmith a few minutes before the fire. Arkhip the blacksmith, everyone agreed, was still alive and was probably the chief, if not sole, instigator of the fire. But Dubrovsky too was under strong suspicion. Kirila Petrovich sent the governor a detailed account of the whole incident, and more legal proceedings began.

It was not long before new reports gave fresh grounds for curiosity and gossip. Brigands appeared, spreading terror throughout the district. Measures taken against them by the authorities proved of no avail. Robberies, each more startling than the one before, followed one after another. There was no safety either on the roads or in the villages. All over the province, in broad daylight, brigands were driving about in troikas, stopping travelers and mail coaches, entering villages, pillaging and torching the houses of landowners. The robber chief gained a reputation for intelligence, daring, and a certain magnanimity. Wondrous tales were told of him; the name of Dubrovsky was on every lip, everyone being convinced that Dubrovsky was indeed the commander of these daring brigands. Most astonishing of all was the fact that Troyekurov's estates were being spared; the brigands had not pillaged a single barn or waylaid a single cart that belonged to him. With his usual arrogance, Troyekurov put this down to the fear he inspired throughout the province, and also to the exceptionally good police force he had organized in his villages. At first his neighbors joked with one another about Troyekurov's presumption, daily expecting uninvited guests to visit Pokrovskoye, an estate where there was certainly plenty for them to loot—but in the end they had no choice but to agree with Troyekurov and admit that even brigands treated him with remarkable respect. Troyekurov was triumphant; every time he heard about a new exploit of Dubrovsky's, he came out with witticisms both about the governor and about the police officers and company commanders from whom Dubrovsky always escaped unharmed.

Meanwhile the 1st of October arrived, the day of the festival—that of Pokrov or the Intercession of the Holy Virgin—after which the church in Troyekurov's village was named. But, before we go on to describe this festival and the events that followed it, we must introduce the reader to characters who are either new to him or her, or else have been mentioned only briefly at the beginning of our tale.

8

The reader, most probably, has already guessed that Kirila Petrovich's daughter, about whom we have so far said only a few words, is the heroine of our tale. At the time of which we are writing she was seventeen and in the full flower of her beauty. Her father loved her to distraction but treated her in his usual capricious manner, one moment attempting to indulge her every least whim, another moment frightening her with his sternness, and sometimes even cruelty. Confident as he was of her affection, he was unable to win her trust. She had grown used to hiding her thoughts and feelings from him, since she never knew how he would respond. She had no friends and had grown up in solitude. The neighbors' wives and daughters seldom visited Kirila Petrovich, whose usual conversation and amusements called more for masculine bonhomie than the presence of ladies. Seldom did our young beauty appear among the guests feasting with Kirila Petrovich. The huge library, consisting mainly of the works of French writers of the eighteenth century, had been placed at her disposal. Her father, who never read anything except *The Perfect Cook*, was unable to guide her in her choice of books, and Masha, after dipping into works of every genre, naturally ended up reading novels. Thus she completed the education begun some time ago by Mam'selle

Mimi, a woman whom Kirila Petrovich had trusted and greatly liked and whom he had been obliged to send off discreetly to another of his estates when the consequences of his friendship with her became too apparent. People had fond memories of Mam'selle Mimi. She was a good-hearted girl and—unlike the other mistresses who replaced one another in quick succession—she had never abused her evident influence on Kirila Petrovich. Kirila Petrovich seemed to have loved her more than the others, and a naughty, dark-eyed little nine-year-old boy, whose southern features recalled those of Mam'selle Mimi, was being brought up in the house as his son, even though a great many other little boys, as like Kirila Petrovich as one drop of water to another, ran about barefoot outside his windows and were regarded as serf-children. Kirila Petrovich had ordered a French tutor to be sent down from Moscow for his little Sasha, and this tutor arrived at the time of the events we are now describing.

The tutor's pleasant appearance and straightforward manner made a favorable impression on Kirila Petrovich. He presented his testimonials, together with a letter from a relative of Troyekurov's at whose house he had served as a tutor for four years. Kirila Petrovich examined everything and was dissatisfied only with the Frenchman's youth—not because he thought this likeable shortcoming indicated a lack of the patience and experience so necessary to anyone in the unfortunate role of tutor, but because he had other doubts, which he resolved to voice to the young man at once. To this end he sent for Masha (Kirila Petrovich did not speak French, and she acted as his interpreter).

"Come here, Masha. Tell this moosieur that yes, I'll take him on, but only on condition he doesn't start chasing after my girls. Or I'll teach him, the son of a bitch...Translate that, Masha."

Masha blushed and, turning to the tutor, said to him in French that her father counted on his modest and proper conduct.

The Frenchman bowed to her and replied that he hoped to earn respect even if he did not win favor.

Masha translated his reply word for word.

"Very good, very good," said Kirila Petrovich. "But he needn't be bothering himself about either favor or respect. His business is to look after Sasha and to teach him grammar and geography. Translate that to him."

Maria Kirilovna softened her father's rudeness in her translation, and Kirila Petrovich dismissed the Frenchman, ordering him to be shown to the wing where a room had been prepared for him.

Masha paid no attention to the young Frenchman. Brought up with the prejudices of an aristocrat, she looked on a tutor as a kind of servant or artisan—and a servant or artisan, in her eyes, was not a man. She noticed neither the general impression she made on Monsieur Desforges, nor his embarrassment, nor his agitation, nor the change in his voice. Several days in a row she came across him fairly often, but without taking any particular notice of him. An unexpected incident showed him in a new light.

There were usually a number of bear cubs being raised in one of the yards; these were one of the chief amusements of the master of Pokrovskoye. When they were very little, they were brought every day into the living room and Kirila Petrovich would play with them for hours on end, setting them against the cats and puppies. When they grew up, they were put on a chain, to await being baited in earnest. Sometimes they were led out in front of the windows of the main house and an empty wine cask studded with nails was rolled towards them; the bear would sniff the cask, touch it cautiously, and hurt its paw; angered, it would push the cask more violently and hurt itself still more. Then it would work itself into a perfect frenzy, growling and flinging itself at the barrel until the object of the poor beast's futile rage was taken away. On other occasions a pair of bears was harnessed to a cart, and visitors, willing or unwilling, were seated in it and sent off who knows where at a gallop. But Kirila Petrovich's favorite prank was the following:

A hungry bear would be locked in an empty room, tethered by a rope to a ring in the wall. The rope ran almost the length of the room, so that only the furthest corner was safe from the attacks of the terrible beast. Some novice would be led to the door of the room, pushed in, and locked inside; the unfortunate victim was then left on his own with the shaggy recluse. The poor visitor, scratched and bleeding, his coat ripped, would quickly discover the safe corner, but he would sometimes have to stand there as long as three hours, flattening himself against the wall while the furious beast, only a couple of steps away, leaped, growled, got up on its hind legs, and vainly struggled to claw him. Such were the noble pastimes of a Russian gentleman!

A few mornings after the tutor's arrival, Troyekurov took it into his head to entertain him, too, with a visit to the bear's room. He sent for him, then led him down some dark corridors; a side door opened, and two servants instantly pushed the Frenchman in and locked the door after him. Recovering from his surprise, the tutor saw the tethered bear; the animal snorted, sniffed from a distance at its visitor, and, standing up on its hind legs, advanced on him. The Frenchman, unruffled, stood his ground and awaited the attack. The bear came close; Desforges took a small pistol from his pocket, held it to the hungry beast's ear, and fired. The bear rolled over. Everyone came running, the door opened, and Kirila Petrovich came in, astonished at this unexpected denouement to his joke. He insistently demanded an explanation: Who had alerted Desforges to the joke about to be played on him? Or what other reason did he have for carrying a loaded pistol in his pocket? He sent for Masha. Masha hurried in and translated her father's questions to the Frenchman.

"I knew nothing of the bear," Desforges replied, "but I always carry a pistol about my person, because I do not intend to endure insults for which, in view of my position, I am unable to demand satisfaction."

Masha looked at him in amazement and translated his words to Kirila Petrovich. Kirila Petrovich made no answer, ordered the bear to be taken out and skinned, then turned to his men and said, "What a fine fellow! He's certainly no coward. No sir!" From that moment he felt a fondness for Desforges, and he never again thought of putting him to the test.

The incident made a still deeper impression on Maria Kirilovna. Her imagination was enthralled: in her mind's eye she kept seeing the dead bear, and Desforges standing calmly over the bear and then calmly conversing with her. She realized that courage and a sense of proper pride were not the exclusive attribute of a single class, and from then on she began to show the young tutor a respect that included more and more warmth of feeling. A certain intimacy arose between them. Masha had a fine voice and real musical ability; Desforges offered to give her lessons. After this, it will be easy enough for the reader to guess that Masha fell in love with him, not yet acknowledging this even to herself.

PART TWO

9

THE GUESTS began to arrive on the eve of the feast day. Some stayed in the manor house or one of its wings, some at the steward's, some at the priest's, and others with the more well-to-do peasants. The stables were full of horses, the yards and barns packed with all kinds of carriages. At nine in the morning the bells began to ring for Mass, and everyone set off for the new stone church that Kirila Petrovich had built and that he embellished with new gifts every year. There was such a crowd of distinguished worshippers that there was no room for anyone else, and the ordinary peasants had to stand on the porch or in the churchyard. Mass had not yet begun; they were waiting for Kirila Petrovich. He arrived in a coach-and-six and solemnly walked to his place, accompanied by Maria Kirilovna. The eyes of both men and women were turned on her—the men marveling at her beauty and the women scrutinizing her dress. The Mass began. The choir was formed from Kirila Petrovich's house serfs, and he himself joined in with them; he prayed, looking neither to left nor to right, and he bowed to the ground with proud humility when the deacon spoke, in a voice as loud as thunder, of the founder of this church.

The Mass came to an end. Kirila Petrovich was first to go up and kiss the cross. Everyone else did the same. Kirila Petrovich's neighbors then paid their respects to him. The ladies surrounded Masha. As he left the church, Kirila Petrovich invited everyone to dine with him; he got into his carriage and set off home. Everyone drove off after him.

Kirila Petrovich's rooms were filling with guests. Every minute new people arrived and could barely push their way through to the master of the house. The ladies sat in a decorous semicircle, all in pearls and diamonds, dressed in costly old-fashioned gowns that had seen better days; the men crowded round the vodka and caviar, raising their voices as they talked and argued. The table in the dining hall had been laid for eighty. The house serfs bustled about, arranging bottles and decanters and straightening tablecloths. At last the butler announced, "Dinner is served," and Kirila Petrovich was first to take his place at the table. The ladies followed him and solemnly took their places, in accord with their age; the young girls huddled together like a timid flock of kid goats, making sure they could all sit next to one another. The men sat down opposite. At the end of the table, beside little Sasha, sat the tutor.

The house serfs began to serve the guests, according to rank; when they were unsure, they followed the principles of Lavater and hardly made a mistake.[14] The clink of plates and spoons mingled with the loud voices of the guests. Kirila Petrovich looked round the table merrily, enjoying to the full the happiness of playing the hospitable host. Just then a coach-and-six drew into the yard. "Who's that?" asked the host. "Anton Pafnutich," answered several voices. The door opened and Anton Pafnutich Spitsyn, a stout man of about fifty with a round pockmarked face adorned by a triple chin, burst into the dining room, bowing, smiling, and already preparing his apologies. "Set a place for him right here," shouted Kirila Petrovich. "Welcome, Anton Pafnutich! Sit down and tell us the meaning of all this: you missed my Mass and now you're late for dinner. It's not like you at all: you're a pious man and you're fond of your food." "I'm sorry," Anton Pafnutich replied, tucking a corner of his napkin into a buttonhole of his pea-green kaftan. "Excuse me, dear sir Kirila Petrovich. I set off in good time but I'd barely gone five miles when the rim of one of my front wheels split in half—what could I do? Fortunately we weren't far from a village, but it still took us three whole hours to drag the carriage there, track down the blacksmith, and patch things up as best we could. There was nothing for it. And I didn't dare take the shortcut across the Kisteniovka wood—I took the roundabout way."

"Oho!" Kirila Petrovich broke in, "I can see you're no hero! And what is it you're so afraid of?"

"What is it I'm afraid of, dear sir Kirila Petrovich? Why, I'm afraid of Dubrovsky! Who knows when one might not fall into his clutches? He's nobody's fool and he doesn't let people off lightly. As for me, he'd skin me twice over."

"And what, Brother, might make him single you out for such an honor?"

"What do you mean, dear sir Kirila Petrovich? Because of the lawsuit against the late Andrey Gavrilovich! Wasn't it I who, for your own satisfaction—that is, in accord with truth and my conscience— testified that the Dubrovskys had no right to the property and were living in Kisteniovka only by virtue of your own generosity? The late Andrey Gavrilovich (may he rest in peace) said he'd get even with me one way or another; might not the son keep his father's word? Until now, God has spared me. So far they've only pillaged one of my barns, but who knows when they might not plunder the house?"

"They'll have a fine time when they do," said Kirila Petrovich. "Your little red-leather coffer must be crammed to the brim."

"What do you mean, my dear sir Kirila Petrovich? It was once, but now it's quite empty."

"Enough of your humbug, Anton Pafnutich! We all know what you're like: what do you ever spend money on? You live like a pig in a sty, you don't receive guests, you fleece your peasants—I'll vow you've been putting away a tidy sum!"

"You are pleased to joke, dear sir Kirila Petrovich," Anton Pafnutich murmured with a smile, "but I swear to you that we're ruined." He then took away the taste of his host's high-handed jokes with a slice of rich pie. Kirila Petrovich decided to let him be; he turned his attention to the new police captain, who had come to the house for the first time and was sitting at the far end of the table, beside the tutor.

"Well, Mr. Captain, are you going to be catching Dubrovsky for us?"

Thrown into a panic, the captain bowed, smiled, stammered, and finally brought out the words, "We'll do our best, Your Excellency."

"Your best, eh? You people have been doing your best for some time now, but not much has come of it yet. But then, why should you want to catch him? Dubrovsky's robberies are a godsend for a police captain: journeys, investigations, expeditions—yes, it all helps feather the nest. Why do away with such a benefactor? Isn't that so, Mr. Captain?"

"That's the absolute truth, Your Excellency," said the police captain, totally confused.

The guests all roared with laughter.

"I like the young fellow's honesty," said Kirila Petrovich, "but it's a pity about our late captain Taras Alexeyevich. Yes, if he hadn't been in the fire, it would be a lot quieter in these parts. But what news of Dubrovsky? When was he last seen?"

"At my house, Kirila Petrovich," came a lady's deep voice. "He dined with me last Tuesday."

All eyes turned towards Anna Savishna Globova, a widow whom everyone loved for her straightforward, kind, and cheerful disposition. The party awaited her story with interest.

"Well, three weeks ago I sent my steward to the post with some money for my young Vanya. I don't spoil my son, and I'm in no position to spoil him even if I wanted to. Still, as you all know, a Guards officer has to take proper care of himself and I share with my Vanya what income I have. And so I sent him two thousand rubles. The thought of Dubrovsky did cross my mind, but I said to myself: It's not far to the town—only five miles—and with God's help the money will get through. And then, come evening—my steward returns on foot, pale-faced and with his clothes all torn. "What's the matter?" I gasp. "What's happened to you?" "Dear ma'am Anna Savishna," he says, "I was robbed by highwaymen. They nearly killed me. Dubrovsky was one of them, he wanted to hang me, but then he took pity on me and let me go—but not without taking everything I had, even the horse and cart." My heart almost stopped: Father in Heaven, I thought, what'll become of my Vanya? But what could I do? I wrote my son another letter; I told him everything and sent him my blessing, without so much as a kopek.

"A week went by, then another week—suddenly a carriage drives into my yard. Some general's asking to see me; I invite him in. In comes a man of about thirty-five, swarthy, black-haired, a moustache and beard, the spitting image of Kulnev.[15] He introduces himself as a friend and comrade of my late husband Ivan Andreyevich's; he was driving past and, knowing I live here, he couldn't not call on his old comrade's widow. I treated him to what food I had in the house; we talked about this and that, and in the end we got to Dubrovsky. 'That's very strange,' he said. 'What I've heard is that Dubrovsky doesn't attack just anyone but only people generally known to be wealthy—and that he's merciful even to them and never strips them of everything. And no one's ever accused him of murder. I wonder if there hasn't been some mischief—pray send for your steward.' I sent for the steward. The man came in; seeing the general, he was dumbfounded. 'So tell me, my good fellow, the story of how Dubrovsky robbed you and wanted to hang you.' My steward began to tremble, and he threw himself at the general's feet. 'Gracious sir, I did wrong—it was the work of the devil—I lied.' 'In that case,' said the general, 'be so kind as to tell the lady just what did happen, and I shall listen.' My steward was speechless. 'Come on,' said the general, 'tell us where you met Dubrovsky!' 'By the two pines, gracious sir, by the two pines.' 'And what did he say to you?' 'He asked me whose man I was, where was I going, and why.' 'And after that?' 'After that he demanded the letter and the money.' 'And then?' 'Then I gave him the letter and the money.' 'And then? What did he do then?' 'Gracious sir, I did wrong.' 'But what did Dubrovsky do?' 'He returned the money and the letter, and he said, "Well, God be with you. Take it to the post."' 'And what did you do?' 'Gracious sir, I did wrong.' 'I'll settle with you later, my dear friend,' said the general menacingly. 'And you, madam, should first order this scoundrel's trunk to be searched, then hand him over to me so I can teach him a lesson. I'd like you to know that Dubrovsky was once a Guards officer himself and it's not his way to do wrong to a comrade.' Well, I had some idea who His Excellency really was, but I thought it best to keep mum. His coachmen tied the steward to the box of the carriage. They found the money; the general had dinner with me and went off straight afterwards, taking the steward with him. The steward was found in the forest the next day, tied to an oak and flogged good and proper."

The entire company, and especially the young ladies, listened to Anna Savishna's story with bated breath. Many of them secretly wished Dubrovsky well, seeing him as a romantic hero; this was especially true of Maria Kirilovna, an ardent dreamer brought up on the mysterious horrors of Mrs. Radcliffe.[16]

"And so you imagine that was Dubrovsky, Anna Savishna?" asked Kirila Petrovich. "You're very much mistaken. I don't know who your visitor was, but it certainly wasn't Dubrovsky."

"What do you mean, my dear sir? Who else but Dubrovsky roams the highways, stopping travelers and searching them?"

"I've no idea, but your visitor certainly wasn't Dubrovsky. I can remember him as a child. His hair may have gone dark since, though it was fair and curly when he was little—but I know for sure that Dubrovsky is five years older than my Masha, and that makes him not thirty-five but around twenty-three."

"Exactly so, Your Excellency," observed the police captain. "I have a description of Vladimir Dubrovsky in my pocket. It says quite precisely that he's in his twenty-third year."

"Ah!" said Kirila Petrovich. "There's an idea. Perhaps you could read us that description. It would be no bad thing if we all knew his distinguishing features. If we happen to run into him, we wouldn't want him slipping away, would we?"

The captain took a rather dirty sheet of paper from his pocket, solemnly unfolded it, and read in a singsong voice: "Distinguishing features of Vladimir Dubrovsky, based upon descriptions given by his former serfs. Age: in his twenty-third year. Height: medium. Complexion: clear. Beard: none. Eyes: brown. Hair: light brown. Nose: straight. Special distinguishing features: none."

"That's all?" asked Kirila Petrovich.

"That's all," replied the captain, folding the paper.

"My congratulations, Mr. Captain. That's quite a document! With distinguishing features like that you'll have no trouble finding Dubrovsky. After all, there aren't so many people of medium height, with light-brown hair, a straight nose, and brown eyes! I'll wager you could talk three full hours with Dubrovsky himself and not realize whom Fate has thrown in your path. There's no denying it, you officers are a smart lot!"

The captain meekly put the document back in his pocket and turned silently to his goose and cabbage. Meanwhile, the servants had been round the table several times, refilling everyone's glasses. Several bottles of Caucasian and Crimean wine had been loudly uncorked and favorably received under the name of champagne; faces were beginning to glow; conversations were becoming louder, merrier, and less coherent.

"No," Kirila Petrovich went on, "we'll never see another captain like the late Taras Alexeyevich! He knew what was what, no one could pull the wool over his eyes. A pity he was burned in the fire—not one of this band would have escaped a man like him. He'd have caught every last one of them; not even Dubrovsky himself could have wriggled or bribed his way out. Taras Alexeyevich would have accepted his bribe all right, but he wouldn't have let him go. Yes, that was the way of the deceased. Well, there's nothing for it—seems I'll have to take the law into my own hands and go after the brigands with my own men. I'll begin by detailing twenty men to scour the robbers' wood. My men aren't cowards, every one of them would take on a bear single-handed, they're not the sort to run from robbers."

"How is your bear, dear sir Kirila Petrovich?" asked Anton Pafnutich, reminded by these words of his shaggy acquaintance and of certain jests of which he had once been the victim. "Misha has departed this life,"[17] replied Kirila Petrovich. "He died a glorious death, at the hands of the enemy. There sits his conqueror." And Kirila Petrovich pointed at Desforges. "You should commission a portrait of my Frenchman. He has avenged your . . . begging your pardon—do you remember?"

"How could I not remember?" said Anton Pafnutich, scratching himself. "I remember very well. So Misha's dead—I'm sorry, upon my word I'm sorry! What a joker he was! How quick-witted! You'll never find another bear like him. And why did moosieur kill him?"

Kirila Petrovich began with great pleasure to relate the bold deed carried out by his Frenchman, for he possessed the fortunate ability to take pride in everything around him. The guests listened attentively to the tale of Misha's death and looked with amazement at Desforges, who, not suspecting that the subject of the conversation was his own bravery, was sitting quietly at the table, now and again admonishing his restive pupil.

The dinner, which had lasted about three hours, came to an end. The host put his napkin on the table, and everyone got to their feet and went to the drawing room, where coffee and cards awaited them, and yet more of the drinking so splendidly begun in the dining hall.

10

Around seven in the evening some of the guests wanted to go but the host, merry from punch, ordered the gates to be locked and declared that no one would be allowed to leave the house until morning. Soon afterwards the band struck up, the doors to the great hall were opened, and dancing began. The host and his cronies sat in one corner, drinking glass after glass and delighting in the gaiety of the young. The old women played cards. As always, except where some cavalry brigade is quartered, there were fewer gentlemen than ladies, and every man fit to dance was recruited. The tutor especially distinguished himself: he danced more than anyone, all the young ladies choosing him and finding him extremely easy to waltz with. He whirled round several times with Maria Kirilovna, and the other young ladies made little jokes as they watched. At last, around midnight, the tired host brought the dancing to an end, ordered supper to be served, and himself retired to bed.

With Kirila Petrovich out of the way, the guests felt more at ease and more animated. Gentlemen ventured to sit next to ladies. The young girls laughed and exchanged whispers with their neighbors; the ladies talked loudly across the table. The men drank, argued, and roared with laughter—in short, it was a most enjoyable meal that left behind many a pleasant memory.

Only one person did not share in the general merriment: Anton Pafnutich sat there gloomy and silent, eating abstractedly and looking extremely anxious. The talk of brigands had troubled his imagination. We shall soon see that he had reason enough to fear them.

In calling God to witness that his little red-leather coffer was empty, Anton Pafnutich had not lied or sinned: his little coffer was indeed empty, the money he kept in it having been transferred to a leather pouch he wore against his chest, beneath his shirt. Only through this precaution was he able to calm his constant fearfulness and his mistrust of everyone around him. Obliged to spend the night in someone else's house, he was afraid of being assigned some remote room that could easily be broken into by thieves. He looked around for a reliable companion, and in the end he chose Desforges. Desforges's obvious physical strength and—still more—the courage he had shown on encountering the bear, whom poor Anton Pafnutich was himself unable to remember without trembling, decided his choice. When they got up from the table, Anton Pafnutich began circling about near the young Frenchman, coughing and clearing his throat; in the end he turned to him with this request: "Hm, hm, could I possibly, moosieur, spend the night in your little room, because, you see—"

"*Que désire monsieur?*"[18] asked Desforges, bowing politely.

"Oh, how unfortunate it is, moosieur, that you have not yet learned Russian. *Je veux, moi, chez vous coucher.*[19] Do you understand?"

"*Monsieur, très volontiers,*" said Desforges. "*Veuillez donner des ordres en conséquence.*"[20]

Very pleased with his fluency in the French tongue, Anton Pafnutich went off at once to tell the servants.

The guests began wishing one another good night and retiring to their appointed rooms; Anton Pafnutich and the tutor went across to the wing. It was a dark night. Desforges lit the way with a lantern; Anton Pafnutich walked behind in tolerable spirits, occasionally pressing his secret pouch to his breast to check that his money was still there.

When they reached the room, the tutor lit a candle and they undressed. At the same time, Anton Pafnutich paced around, checking the locks and windows and shaking his head, disheartened by what he found. The door was closed only by a latch, and the windows had not yet been fitted with their second frames.[21] He tried to complain about this to Desforges, but his knowledge of the French tongue proved inadequate for a discussion of such complex matters; the Frenchman did not understand him and Anton Pafnutich had no choice but to stop complaining. The two beds were opposite one another; the men lay down, and the tutor blew out the candle.

"Pourquoi vous touchez, pourquoi vous touchez?"[22] Anton Pafnutich called out, doing his best to conjugate the Russian for the verb *to extinguish* as if it were French. "I cannot *dormir* in the dark."[23] Not understanding his exclamations, Desforges wished him good night.

"Damned heathen!" Anton Pafnutich muttered, wrapping himself in his blanket. "Why does he have to go and blow out the candle? How's that going to help? Moosieur, moosieur," he went on, "*je veux avec vous parler.*"[24] But the Frenchman said nothing and soon began to snore.

"Snoring brute of a Frenchman!" thought Anton Pafnutich. "I'll be lucky if I get any sleep at all myself. Any moment now thieves will walk in through an unlocked door, or they'll climb through the window—and not even a cannon's going to wake this brute!"

"Moosieur! Moosieur! The devil take you!"

Anton Pafnutich fell silent; fatigue and the effects of alcohol gradually got the better of his fears. He dozed off and soon sank into deep slumber.

A strange awakening was in store for him. Still asleep, he felt that someone was gently pulling at his shirt collar. Anton Pafnutich opened his eyes and saw Desforges standing over him in the pale light of an autumn morning: the Frenchman was holding a pocket pistol in one hand and unfastening the precious pouch with the other. Anton Pafnutich's heart stood still.

"Qu'est-ce que c'est, moosieur, *qu'est-ce que c'est?"*[25] he brought out in a trembling voice.

"Shh! Be quiet!" the tutor replied in the purest Russian. "Be quiet, or you're done for. I am Dubrovsky."

11

We shall now ask the reader of our tale for permission to explain these last events by certain previous incidents that we have not yet had time to relate.

In a corner of the post-station building whose postmaster we have already mentioned, there sat a traveler whose meek, patient air showed him to be either a member of the intelligentsia or a foreigner—a man, anyway, who had no rights at post stations. His trap stood outside in the yard, waiting for its wheels to be greased. In it lay a small suitcase, proof of his restricted circumstances. The traveler asked for neither tea nor coffee but just looked through the window and whistled—to the great displeasure of the postmaster's wife, who was sitting behind the partition.

"So the Lord's sent us a whistler," she said under her breath. "May he be struck dumb, the damned heathen!"

"Why?" asked the postmaster. "Where's the harm in it? Let him whistle!"

"The harm in it?" his wife repeated crossly. "Don't you know the saying?"

"What saying? That whistling blows away money? No, Pakhomovna. Makes no difference to us. There's no money here to be blown away."

"Send him on his way, Sidorych. What are you keeping him for? Give him some horses and let him go to the devil."

"He can wait, Pakhomovna. I've only three troikas in the stables; the fourth is resting. Who knows—some better traveler may turn up. No, I'm not risking my neck for a Frenchman. Ha! What did I say? Here's one right now. Aha! And at a gallop! Could be a general!"

A carriage stopped by the porch. A servant jumped down from the box and opened the door, and a moment later a young man in a military greatcoat and a white cap came in; the servant followed, carrying a small box which he placed on the windowsill.

"Horses!" said the officer imperiously.

"At once," said the postmaster. "May I have your traveling papers?"

"I don't have any. I'm not taking the main road. Do you not recognize me?"

The postmaster bustled around and rushed out to hurry up the coachmen. The young man paced up and down the room, then went behind the partition and quietly asked the postmaster's wife who the other traveler was.

"God only knows," she replied. "Some Frenchman or other. Five hours now he's been waiting for horses and whistling. I've had enough of the wretch."

The young man began to talk to the traveler in French.

"May I inquire where you are going?" he asked.

"To the nearest town," the Frenchman replied, "and from there to a landowner who's engaged me by letter as a tutor. I thought I'd be there today, but Monsieur Postmaster seems to have decided otherwise. It's not so easy to get horses in this country, Monsieur Officer."

"And which of the local landowners are you going to be working for?" asked the officer.

"Monsieur Troyekurov."

"Troyekurov? What kind of a man is this Troyekurov?"

"*Ma foi, mon officier*,[26] I've not heard much good of him. They say he's a proud and headstrong gentleman and that he treats his subordinates cruelly. No one can get on with him, everyone trembles at the mere mention of his name, and he doesn't stand upon ceremony with tutors. He's already flogged two to death."

"Heaven help us! And you're resolved to work for a monster like that?"

"What can I do, monsieur officer? He's offering me a good salary—three thousand rubles a year, with board and lodging. Maybe I'll be luckier than the others. My mother's an old woman; I'll be sending off half of my salary for her to live on, and within five years I'll have saved enough from the other half to secure my independence. Then, *bonsoir*—I'll be off to Paris to set myself up in business."

"Does anyone in Troyekurov's house know you?"

"No," said the tutor. "He heard of me through a friend of his in

Moscow, whose cook, a compatriot of mine, recommended me. I should say that I first intended to work not as a tutor but as a pastry chef, but I was told that in your country the calling of tutor is a great deal more profitable."

The officer stood thinking.

"Listen," he said, "how would you feel if, instead of this position, someone offered you ten thousand rubles in cash on condition you return at once to Paris?"

The Frenchman looked at the officer in amazement, smiled, and shook his head.

"Your horses are ready," said the postmaster, coming into the room. The servant repeated this.

"Thank you," said the officer. "Leave the room for a moment." The postmaster and the servant both left. "I'm not joking," he continued in French. "I can give you ten thousand rubles. In return I ask only for your absence and your papers." With these words he opened his box and took out several bundles of banknotes.

The Frenchman gaped. He didn't know what to think.

"My absence . . . my papers," he repeated in amazement. "Here are my papers . . . But you're joking. What use are my papers to you?"

"That's no concern of yours. I'm asking you: Do you agree, or not?"

The Frenchman, still unable to believe his ears, handed his papers to the young officer, who quickly looked through them.

"Your passport . . . Good. Letter of recommendation, let me see . . . Birth certificate, splendid. Here's your money, then—you can go back home. Goodbye."

The Frenchman stood rooted to the spot.

The officer came back.

"I almost forgot the most important thing. Give me your word of honor that all this will remain between ourselves. Your word of honor."

"My word of honor," the Frenchman replied. "But what about my papers? How will I get by without them?"

"Report in the first town you come to that you were robbed by Dubrovsky. The authorities will believe you and give you the necessary attestation. Goodbye. God grant you return quickly to Paris and find your mother in good health."

Dubrovsky left the room, got into his carriage and galloped off.

The postmaster looked out of the window, and when the carriage was out of sight he turned to his wife and exclaimed, "You know what, Pakhomovna? That was Dubrovsky!"

The postmistress rushed to the window, but it was too late: Dubrovsky was far away. She began scolding her husband:

"Have you no fear of the Lord, Sidorych? Why didn't you tell me before? I could have caught a glimpse of Dubrovsky! He won't be back now till kingdom come. Shameless, that's what I call you, shameless!"

The Frenchman still stood rooted to the spot. His agreement with the officer, the money—all seemed like a dream. But the bundles of banknotes were there in his pocket, eloquently confirming that this astonishing event had truly happened.

He resolved to hire horses to the nearest town. The coachman drove at a slow pace, and night fell before they arrived.

Before reaching the town gate, where there was a tumbledown sentry box but no sentry, the Frenchman ordered the driver to stop, got out of the trap, and continued on foot, explaining through gestures that the driver was to keep the trap and the suitcase by way of a tip. The driver was as much astonished by such generosity as the Frenchman himself had been by Dubrovsky's proposal. But, concluding that the dumb foreigner had gone out of his mind, he thanked him with a low bow and, considering it wiser not to enter the town, made his way to a certain house of entertainment, whose landlord he knew exceedingly well. There he spent the entire night. In the morning he set off back home with the three horses but no trap and no suitcase; he had a swollen face and red eyes.

Having obtained the Frenchman's papers, Dubrovsky boldly presented himself, as we have seen, to Troyekurov and settled into his house. Whatever his secret intentions (and we shall learn these in due course), his conduct was blameless. True, he did not greatly concern himself with little Sasha's education. He gave the boy free rein, letting him get up to all kinds of mischief, and he was far from exacting with regard to lessons, doing only what was necessary to keep up appearances; he did, however, devote himself with great diligence to the musical progress of his other pupil, often sitting with her at the piano for hours on end. Everybody loved the young tutor: Kirila Petrovich—for his quick daring when they were out hunting; Maria Kirilovna—for his boundless zeal and timid attentiveness; Sasha—for treating him indulgently when he got up to mischief; the servants—for his kindness and for a generosity that seemed out of keeping with his position. He himself seemed to have grown attached to the whole family and to consider himself one of its members.

About a month had gone by between his taking up the calling of tutor and the festivities we have described—and no one suspected that the modest young Frenchman might really be the terrible brigand whose name alone was enough to inspire terror in all the local landowners. Dubrovsky had not once left Pokrovskoye, but rumors about his robberies continued to spread, thanks to the inventive imagination of those who dwell in the country; though it may also have been that his band continued their activities even in the absence of their chief.

Passing the night in the same room as a man whom he had reason to consider his personal enemy and one of the principal authors of his misfortunes, Dubrovsky was unable to resist temptation. He knew about the existence of the pouch and he decided to gain possession of it. We have seen how he amazed poor Anton Pafnutich by his sudden transformation from tutor to brigand.

At nine o'clock in the morning, the guests who had passed the night at Pokrovskoye began to gather one after another in the drawing room, where a samovar was already boiling; seated before it was Maria Kirilovna in her morning dress, while Kirila Petrovich, in a flannelette frock coat and slippers, was drinking tea from a cup as broad as a slop basin. The last to appear was Anton Pafnutich; he was so pale and appeared so distressed that everyone was startled by the mere sight of him and Kirila Petrovich inquired after his health. Anton Pafnutich answered incoherently and kept looking in horror at the tutor, who was sitting there as if nothing had happened. A few minutes later a servant came in and announced that Anton Pafnutich's carriage was ready; he hurried to take his leave and, in spite of his host's protestations, rushed out of the room and drove off straightaway. No one could understand what was the matter with him, and Kirila Petrovich decided he had overeaten. After morning tea and a farewell luncheon, the other guests began to disperse; soon Pokrovskoye was empty and everything resumed its normal course.

12

Several days passed, and nothing worthy of note occurred. Life at Pokrovskoye was the same as ever. Kirila Petrovich went out hunting every day, while Maria Kirilovna kept herself occupied with reading, going for walks, and—most important of all—music lessons. She was beginning to understand her own heart and, with involuntary irritation, to acknowledge that it was not indifferent to the fine qualities of the young Frenchman. He for his part never stepped beyond the bounds of respect and strict propriety, thus soothing her pride and timorous doubts. She surrendered ever more trustingly to a captivating routine. She felt listless without Desforges; and when they were together, she gave him her full attention, wanting to know his opinion about everything and always agreeing with him. She may not yet have been in love but it was clear that, at the first chance obstacle or sudden vicissitude of fate, the flame of passion would flare up in her heart.

One day Maria went into the hall, where her tutor was waiting for her, and was surprised to see a look of confusion on his pale face. She opened the piano and sang a few notes, but Dubrovsky excused himself and broke off the lesson, saying he had a headache. Closing the music book, he slipped a note into her hand. Maria Kirilovna, having no time to think, took the note and at once wished she hadn't— but Dubrovsky was no longer there. She went to her room, unfolded the note and read, "Come at seven o'clock to the arbor beside the stream. It is essential that I speak to you."

This greatly excited her curiosity. She had long been expecting him to confess his feelings, wanting and fearing this at the same time. It would be pleasing to hear confirmation of what she imagined, but she felt it would be improper for her to listen to a confession of love from a man who could never, because of his station in life, hope to win her hand. She decided to keep the tryst, but she was still uncertain about one thing: how to receive this declaration. Should she respond with aristocratic indignation, friendly remonstrances, light-hearted banter, or wordless sympathy? In the meantime she kept looking every minute at the clock. It grew dark; candles were lit; Kirila Petrovich sat down to a game of Boston with neighbors who had driven over. The dining-room clock struck a quarter to seven, and Maria Kirilovna quietly went out onto the porch, looked in every direction, and ran into the garden.

The night was dark, the sky was covered with clouds, and it was impossible to make anything out even two yards away, but Maria Kirilovna walked through the dark, along paths she knew, and was close to the arbor in less than a minute. She stopped, wanting to catch her breath, so that she could meet Desforges with an air of unhurried indifference. But there he was, standing before her.

"Thank you," he said in a quiet, sad voice, "for not denying my request. I should have been in despair if you had not come."

Maria Kirilovna replied with a sentence she had prepared in advance: "I hope you will not give me cause to regret my forbearance."

He said nothing; he seemed to be plucking up his courage.

"Circumstances require . . . I must leave you," he said finally. "Soon, perhaps, you will hear . . . But I owe you an explanation before we part."

Maria Kirilovna did not reply. She heard these words as a preface to the confession she was expecting.

"I am not what you think," he went on, bowing his head. "I am not the Frenchman Desforges. I am Dubrovsky."

Maria Kirilovna shrieked.

"Don't be frightened, for the love of God. You mustn't be afraid of my name. Yes, I am the unfortunate man whom your father has deprived of his last crust of bread; I have been driven out of my family home to become a highway robber. But neither on your account nor on his account do you have anything to fear from me. It is all over. I have pardoned him. And it is you—I must tell you—who saved him. My first bloody deed was to have been directed against your father. I was walking up and down beside his house, deciding where the fire should break out, which way to enter his bedroom, how to cut off his ways of escape—and then you passed by, like a heavenly vision, and my heart was overcome. I understood that the house where you live is sacred and that no one related to you by ties of blood can ever be accursed to me. I renounced vengeance as madness. For days on end I wandered about near the gardens of Pokrovskoye, hoping to glimpse your white dress in the distance. I followed you in your carefree walks; I stole from bush to bush, happy in the thought that I was guarding you, that no danger could threaten you where I was secretly present. At last an opportunity arose. I came to live in your house. These three weeks have been a time of happiness for me. Their memory will be the joy of my sad life. Today I have received news that makes it impossible for me to stay here longer. I am parting from you today... now... But first I had to speak openly to you, so you won't curse me or despise me. Think now and again of Dubrovsky. Be assured that he was born for another destiny, that his soul knew how to love you, that never—"

Just then there was a quiet whistle, and Dubrovsky fell silent. He seized her hand and pressed it to his burning lips. The whistle was repeated.

"Farewell," said Dubrovsky. "They're calling me. A minute's delay could be my downfall." He walked away; Maria Kirilovna remained motionless. Dubrovsky came back and took her hand again.

"If ever," he said in a tender, touching voice, "if ever misfortune befalls you and you have no one to help or protect you, will you promise to turn to me—so I can do everything in my power to save you? Will you promise not to scorn my devotion?"

Maria Kirilovna wept silently. There was a third whistle.

"You will be my downfall!" cried Dubrovsky. "I will not leave you until you give me an answer. Do you promise or not?"

"I promise," whispered the poor beauty.

Agitated by her tryst with Dubrovsky, Maria Kirilovna began to make her way back to the house. The servants all seemed to be running about; the house was in commotion; there were a lot of people in the yard; a troika stood by the porch. She heard Kirila Petrovich's voice from some way away and hurried inside, fearful lest her absence be noticed. Kirila Petrovich went up to her in the main hall. His guests were standing around the police captain—our old acquaintance—and showering him with questions. Dressed for the road and armed from head to toe, the police captain was answering with a mysterious and preoccupied air.

"Where've you been, Masha?" asked Kirila Petrovich. "You haven't seen Monsieur Desforges, have you?" Only with difficulty did Masha manage to say no.

"Would you believe it?" Kirila Petrovich went on. "The police captain's come to arrest him. He insists that Desforges is really Dubrovsky."

"The distinguishing features tally exactly, Your Excellency," said the police captain respectfully.

"Hm, dear brother!" said Kirila Petrovich. "I'll tell you where to go with your distinguishing features. You're not having my Frenchman until I've looked into the matter myself. How can you believe a lying coward like Anton Pafnutich? He must have just dreamed that the tutor wanted to rob him. Why didn't he say anything about it to me at the time?"

"The Frenchman gave him quite a fright, Your Excellency. He made him swear to keep silent."

"It's a pack of lies," said Kirila Petrovich. "I'll clear the whole thing up in a moment...Where's the tutor?" he asked a servant who had just come in.

"He can't be found anywhere, sir."

"Find him then!" shouted Troyekurov, starting to feel uncertain. "Let me have a look at these distinguishing features of yours," he went on. The police captain handed him a piece of paper. "Hm, hm, twenty-three years of age. Maybe—but that doesn't prove very much by itself. Where's the tutor?"

"He can't be found anywhere," was the answer once more. Kirila Petrovich was now feeling anxious. And Maria Kirilovna was neither alive nor dead.

"You're pale, Masha," said her father. "Are you frightened?"

"No, Papa," she replied. "I just have a headache."

"Go off to your room, Masha, and don't be anxious." Masha kissed his hand and hurried off to her room; there she threw herself on the bed and burst into hysterical sobs. The maidservants ran in, undressed her, and, with the help of cold water and every possible kind of smelling salt, managed to calm her down and put her to bed. She fell asleep.

The Frenchman had still not been found. Kirila Petrovich paced up and down the room, ominously whistling, "Thunder of Victory, Resound!" The guests whispered among themselves; the police captain was beginning to look foolish; the Frenchman was nowhere to be seen. He must have had time to escape, he must have been warned. But how, and by whom? That remained a mystery.

The clock struck eleven, but no one was thinking of sleep. In the end Kirila Petrovich said crossly to the police captain, "Well then? You're not going to stay here till daylight, are you? My house isn't a tavern. You'll have to be smarter than this, my good man, to catch Dubrovsky—if that's who it was. Go back home and see if you can move a bit quicker next time...And you can all go home too," he went on, turning to his guests. "Order your carriages, I want to go to bed."

In this ungracious manner Troyekurov saw off his guests.

13

Time went by with no incident worthy of note. At the beginning of the following summer, however, life at Pokrovskoye changed in a number of ways.

About twenty miles from Pokrovskoye lay a fine estate called Arbatovo. Prince Vereisky, the owner, had lived for a long time in foreign lands; his estate had been managed by a retired major, and there had been no commerce between it and Pokrovskoye. But at the end of May the prince returned from abroad and came to live on his estate, which he had never before set eyes on. Accustomed as he was to the dissipations of society, he could not endure solitude, and so, three days after his arrival, he went over to dine with Troyekurov, with whom he had at one time been acquainted.

The prince was about fifty years of age, but he looked much older. Excesses of all kinds had undermined his health and stamped him with their indelible mark. His outward appearance, however, was attractive, even distinguished, and a life spent in society had endowed him with a certain charm, especially in his dealings with women. He had a perpetual need for distraction, and he was perpetually bored. Kirila Petrovich was extremely gratified by his visit, looking on it as a mark of respect from a man who knew the world; in accord with his usual habit, he treated the prince to a tour of his estate, including the kennels. But the prince almost choked in the canine atmosphere and rushed out, pressing a scented handkerchief to his nose. The old-fashioned garden with its clipped limes, rectangular pond, and formal paths was not to his taste; he loved English gardens and what people called nature, but he complimented Troyekurov and professed to be delighted; then a servant came and announced that dinner was served. They went in. The prince was limping, exhausted by the walk, and wishing he hadn't come to Pokrovskoye.

But they were met in the dining hall by Maria Kirilovna, and the old philanderer was struck by her beauty. Troyekurov seated his guest beside her. Animated by her presence, the prince was good company, and he managed to capture her attention several times with his interesting stories. After dinner Kirila Petrovich suggested they go out for a ride, but the prince excused himself, pointing to his velvet boots and joking about his gout; he would prefer to go for a drive, so as not to be separated from his charming companion. A carriage was prepared. The two old men and the young beauty got in and drove off.

The conversation never flagged. Maria Kirilovna was enjoying the merry and flattering compliments of a man of the world when Vereisky suddenly turned to Kirila Petrovich and asked about a burned-down building: did it belong to him? Kirila Petrovich frowned; the memories stirred by this burned-down estate were unpleasant. He replied that the land was now his, but that it had once belonged to Dubrovsky.

"To Dubrovsky?" Vereisky repeated. "The famous brigand?"

"To his father," Troyekurov replied, "who was something of a brigand himself." "And what's become of our Rinaldo?[27] Is he still alive? Has he been captured yet?"

"He's alive and at large. And as long as our police captains make common cause with our robbers, he isn't going to be captured. By the way, Prince, didn't he pay a visit to your Arbatovo?"

"Yes, I think he did some burning or plundering last year. But don't you think, Maria Kirilovna, it would be entertaining to make a closer acquaintance with this romantic hero?"

"Pah!" said Troyekurov. "She's acquainted with him already: he gave her music lessons for three whole weeks. He didn't, thank God, exact any payment." And Kirila Petrovich began to tell the story of his Frenchman. Maria Kirilovna was sitting on thorns. Vereisky listened with deep interest, declared it all very strange, and changed the subject. On their return to the house, he ordered his carriage; in spite of Kirila Petrovich's repeated entreaties to stay the night, he left immediately after tea. Before this, however, he invited Kirila Petrovich and Maria Kirilovna to pay him a visit, and the haughty Troyekurov accepted; taking into account his princely title, his two stars, and the three thousand serfs of his ancestral estate, he looked on Prince Vereisky as to some degree his equal.

Two days after this visit, Kirila Petrovich set off with his daughter to call on Prince Vereisky. As they approached Arbatovo, he couldn't but admire the clean and cheerful-looking huts of the peasants and the stone manor house built in the style of an English castle. In front of the house stretched a lush green meadow on which Swiss cows were grazing, tinkling their little bells. An extensive park surrounded the house on all sides. The host met his visitors on the porch and gave his arm to the young beauty. They entered a magnificent dining hall, where the table was set for three. The prince led his guests to a window, from which there was a charming view. Not far away lay the Volga; loaded barges floated past under full sail; now and again could be seen the small fishing boats so expressively known as *dushegubki*, or coffin-floats. Beyond the river were hills and fields, with a few villages animating the landscape. The three of them went on to inspect the gallery of paintings that the prince had purchased while traveling in foreign parts. The prince explained the subject of each picture to Maria Kirilovna, told her about the painters, and pointed out the merits and shortcomings of their work. He spoke about the paintings with feeling and imagination, not in the conventional language of a pedant. Maria Kirilovna listened to him with pleasure. They went to dine. Troyekurov did full justice both to the wines of his Amphitryon[28] and to the artistry of the chef, and Maria Kirilovna felt not a trace of shyness or constraint as she talked to a man she was seeing for only the second time in her life. After dinner the host invited his guests into the garden. They drank coffee on the shore of a broad lake dotted with islands. A brass band struck up; a six-oared boat appeared, then moored just beside the arbor. They went out onto the lake, rowing past the islands and stopping at some of them; on one they found a marble statue, on another a secluded cave, on a third a monument with a mysterious inscription; the young girl's curiosity was piqued by this—and not altogether satisfied by the prince's courteous reticence; imperceptibly, time passed; it began to get dark. The prince hurried his guests back, pleading the evening chill and the dew. He asked Maria Kirilovna to play the role of hostess in the home of an old bachelor. She poured out the tea, listening to the inexhaustible stories of the amiable raconteur; suddenly they heard a bang, and the sky was illuminated by a rocket. The prince handed Maria Kirilovna a shawl and led her and Troyekurov out onto the balcony. Many-colored lights flared up in the darkness, spun round, rose up like sheaves of grain, like palm trees or fountains, fell like showers of rain or stars, faded and flared up again. Maria Kirilovna was as happy as a child. Prince Vereisky was delighted by her pleasure, and Troyekurov was much gratified: he took *tous les frais*[29] as a sign of the prince's respect, of his desire to please him.

Their supper was in no way less excellent than their dinner. The guests retired to the rooms made ready for them, and in the morning they took leave of their amiable host, all promising to meet again before long.

14

Maria Kirilovna was in her room, sitting by an open window at her embroidery frame. She did not confuse her silks like Konrad's mistress, who, in her amorous distraction, embroidered a rose in green.[30] Beneath Maria Kirilovna's needle, the canvas faultlessly repeated the patterns of the original; her thoughts, however, were far away.

Suddenly a hand was thrust silently through the window; someone placed a letter on the embroidery frame and was gone before Maria Kirilovna could recover from her surprise. Just then a servant entered and called her to Kirila Petrovich. Trembling, she hid the letter under her kerchief and hurried to her father's study.

Kirila Petrovich was not alone. Prince Vereisky was sitting with him. When Maria Kirilovna appeared, the prince stood up and bowed to her in silence, with an awkwardness that was unlike him.

"Come here, Masha," said Kirila Petrovich. "I have some news which, I hope, will make you happy. Here is a suitor for you; the prince is asking for your hand."

Masha was dumbfounded; her face turned deathly pale. She said nothing. The prince went up to her, took her hand, and asked, visibly moved, if she would consent to make him happy.

"Consent, yes, of course she consents," said Kirila Petrovich. "But you know, prince, how difficult it is for a girl to pronounce that word. Well, children, kiss one another and be happy."

Masha stood motionless; the old prince kissed her hand; tears ran down her pale face. The prince frowned slightly.

"Off with you now, off with you," said Kirila Petrovich. "Dry your tears and come back bright and happy... They all weep when they're betrothed," he went on, turning to Vereisky, "seems it's a way of theirs. And now, prince, let us talk business—that is, about the dowry."

Maria Kirilovna eagerly took advantage of this permission to withdraw. She ran to her room, locked herself in, and let her tears flow freely, imagining herself as the wife of the old prince; he had become repulsive and hateful to her. Marriage was as frightening as the executioner's block, as the grave. "No, no," she repeated in despair, "I'd rather die, I'd rather go to a convent, I'd rather marry Dubrovsky." At this point she remembered the letter and avidly began to read it, sensing it must be from him. It was indeed in his hand, and it contained only these words: "This evening, ten o'clock, the same place."

15

The moon was shining; it was a quiet July night; now and then a breeze got up and a gentle rustle passed through the garden.

Like a light shadow, the young beauty drew near the meeting place. There was no one to be seen. Suddenly, from behind the arbor, Dubrovsky appeared before her.

"I know everything," he said in a quiet, sad voice. "Remember your promise."

"You are offering me your protection," said Masha. "But—please don't be angry—your protection frightens me. How can you help me?"

"I could rid you of a hateful man."

"For the love of God, don't touch him. Don't dare to touch him if you love me. I don't want to be the cause of some horror."

"I won't touch him; your wish is sacred to me. He owes his life to you. No evil deed will ever be committed in your name. You must remain pure even though I commit crimes. But how can I save you from a cruel father?"

"There is still hope. I hope to move him with my tears and my despair. He is obstinate, but he loves me very much."

"Don't put your trust in empty hopes. In your tears he will see only the usual timidity and revulsion common to all young women marrying not for love but out of prudent calculation. What if he takes it into his head to make you happy in spite of yourself? What if you are led to the altar by force, handed over forever to the power of an aged husband?"

"Then—then we have no choice. Come for me—I shall be your wife."

Dubrovsky trembled; his pale face flushed crimson, then at once turned paler than before. He remained silent for a long time, his head bowed.

"Gather all the strength of your soul, implore your father, throw yourself at his feet, picture to him all the horror of the future, your youth fading away beside a decrepit and debauched old man, and do not shrink from speaking a cruel truth. Say that, if he remains implacable, you will find a terrible protection. Say that wealth will not bring you even one moment of happiness; luxury comforts only the poor—and only for a brief moment before they grow accustomed to it. Don't give up, don't be afraid of his anger or his threats as long as there remains even a shadow of hope. For the love of God, don't give up. But if there's really no other way..."

Dubrovsky buried his face in his hands; he seemed to be choking. Masha was weeping.

"What a wretched, wretched fate," he said with a bitter sigh. "I was ready to give my life for you; touching your hand, even seeing you in the distance, was ecstasy for me. And now, when there is an opportunity to clasp you to my agitated heart and say, 'My angel, let us die together!' I must beware of bliss, unhappy man that I am. I must thrust it away with all my strength. I dare not fall at your feet and thank heaven for an inexplicable and undeserved reward. Oh, how I should hate the man who... But I can feel that my heart has no room now for hatred."

He gently put his arm round her slim waist and gently drew her to his heart. She leaned her head trustingly on the shoulder of the young brigand. They were both silent.

Time flew. "I must go," said Masha at last. Dubrovsky seemed to wake from a trance. He took her hand and placed a ring on her finger.

"If you resolve to turn to me," he said, "bring this ring here and drop it into the hollow of this oak. I shall know what to do."

He kissed her hand and disappeared among the trees.

16

Prince Vereisky's proposal was no longer a secret in the neighborhood. People offered their congratulations to Kirila Petrovich, and preparations began for the wedding. Day after day Masha put off making any decisive statement. In the meantime, her manner towards her elderly suitor was cold and constrained. The prince was not troubled by this. He did not require love, being satisfied with her silent consent.

But time was passing. Masha finally resolved to act, and she wrote a letter to Prince Vereisky; she tried to awaken a sense of magnanimity in his heart, openly confessing that she felt not the slightest affection towards him and begging him to renounce his suit and so protect her from her father's power. She quietly slipped the letter into Prince Vereisky's hand; he read it when he was alone, and he was not in the least moved by the frank words of his betrothed. On the contrary, he thought it best to bring forward the date of the wedding; with that in mind, he showed the letter to his future father-in-law.

Kirila Petrovich was enraged; only with difficulty did the prince persuade him not to reveal to Masha that he had seen her letter. Kirila Petrovich agreed not to speak about it to her, but he, too, considered it best not to waste time and to hold the wedding in two days' time. The prince thought this extremely sensible; he went to his betrothed and told her that her letter had greatly saddened him but that he hoped to win her affection with time: the thought of losing her was more than he could bear, and he did not have the strength to agree to his own death sentence. After that he respectfully kissed her hand and left, saying not a word about Kirila Petrovich's decision.

But his carriage had barely left before her father went into her room and commanded her point-blank to be ready the next day. Maria Kirilovna, already upset by what Prince Vereisky had said, burst into tears and threw herself at her father's feet.

"Dearest Papa!" she cried pitifully. "Don't destroy me, Papa! I don't love the prince, I don't want to be his wife."

"What do you mean?" Kirila Petrovich asked harshly. "All this time you have remained silent and been quite agreeable—but now, with everything decided, you turn capricious and say you've changed your mind. Don't play the fool with me. It'll get you nowhere."

"Don't destroy me," poor Masha repeated. "Why are you driving me away, giving me to a man I don't love? Are you tired of me? I want to be together with you—the same as always. Sweetest Papa, you'll be sad without me, and still sadder when you remember that I'm unhappy. Don't force me, Papenka, I don't want to be married."

Kirila Petrovich was moved, but he hid his confusion. Pushing her away, he said sternly, "Nonsense, nonsense! I know better than you what you need for your happiness. Your tears are in vain. Your wedding day will be the day after tomorrow."

"The day after tomorrow!" cried Masha. "Dear God! No, no, that's impossible, it can't be. Papenka, listen, if you have made up your mind to destroy me, then I will find a protector, one you would never imagine—and you will see, you will be appalled to see, what you have driven me to."

"What? What?" said Troyekurov. "Threats! Are you threatening me, you impudent wench? Well then, you may find me treating you in a way you find hard to imagine. It won't take us long to find out the name of this protector of yours."

"Vladimir Dubrovsky," Masha replied in despair.

Kirila Petrovich thought she had gone mad; he gazed at her in amazement.

"Very well," he said to her after a silence. "You can wait for whoever you like to deliver you, but you shall wait here in this room. You won't leave it till the hour of your wedding." With these words Kirila Petrovich left the room, locking the door behind him.

The poor girl wept for a long time, imagining all that awaited her, but the stormy scene had relieved her soul and she was able to think more calmly about her situation and the best course of action. The important thing was to escape from a hateful marriage; the life of a brigand's wife seemed paradise in comparison with the fate that had been decided for her. She looked at the ring Dubrovsky had left her. She longed fervently to see him alone and talk everything over once more before the moment of truth. That evening, she sensed, she would find Dubrovsky in the garden, beside the arbor; she resolved to go and wait for him there as soon as it grew dark. Darkness fell. Masha got ready, but her door had been locked. There was a maid outside; she told Masha she had been forbidden to let her out. Masha was under arrest. Deeply humiliated, she sat by the window and stayed there deep into the night without undressing, her eyes fixed on the dark sky. At dawn she dozed off, but her light sleep was disturbed by sad visions, and the rays of the rising sun soon woke her.

17

She awoke, and at once took in the full horror of her position. She rang the bell. A maid came in. In reply to her mistress's questions, she said that Kirila Petrovich had gone to Arbatovo in the evening and come back late; he had given strict instructions that his daughter be kept in her room and not allowed to speak to anyone; otherwise, there was no sign of any particular preparation for the wedding except that the priest had been instructed under no circumstances to leave the village. After telling her this, the maid left Maria Kirilovna and locked the door again.

These words incensed the young prisoner. Her mind seething, her blood boiling, she resolved to let Dubrovsky know everything, and she began to search for a way of delivering the ring to the hollow of the secret oak. Just then a pebble struck her window, clinking against the pane; Maria Kirilovna looked out into the courtyard and saw little Sasha silently trying to attract her attention. Knowing his devotion to her, she was glad to see him. She opened the window.

"Hello, Sasha," she said. "Why are you calling me?"

"I came, sister, to ask if there's anything you need. Papenka is angry, and everyone in the household has been forbidden to take orders from you, but you can ask me anything you like. I'll do what you say."

"Thank you, dear Sashenka! Do you know the old oak tree by the arbor, the one with a hollow?"

"Yes, sister."

"Well then, if you love me, run there as quick as you can and put this ring in the hollow. But don't let anyone see you!"

With these words she threw him the ring and closed the window.

The boy picked up the ring, ran off as fast as his legs would carry him, and was beside the secret oak within three minutes. He stopped, gasping for breath, looked all round, and placed the little ring in the hollow. Having successfully accomplished his task, he was about to go and report back to Masha when a raggedy little boy, red-haired and cross-eyed, darted out from behind the arbor, rushed towards the oak, and put his hand in the hollow. Quicker than a squirrel, Sasha flew at him and seized him with both hands.

"What are you doing here?" he asked fiercely.

"What's it got to do with you?" asked the boy, trying to free himself.

"Leave that ring alone, carrot-top," Sasha shouted, "or you're in trouble!"

By way of an answer, the boy punched him in the face, but Sasha held on, shouting at the top of his voice, "Thieves! Thieves! Help! Help!"

The boy struggled to get away. He looked a couple of years older than Sasha, and he was much stronger; but Sasha was the more agile. They fought for several minutes, until the red-headed boy finally got the upper hand. He threw Sasha to the ground and seized him round the throat.

But just then a powerful hand grabbed him by his red, bristly hair, and Stepan the gardener lifted Sasha a good foot clear of the ground.

"Ginger brute!" said the gardener. "How dare you hit the young master?"

Sasha quickly leaped to his feet and got his breath back.

"You had me under the armpits," he said. "Otherwise you'd never have been able to throw me. Give me the ring now and clear off."

"Not likely," said the red-headed boy, suddenly spinning round and freeing his bristles from Stepan's grip. He sped off but Sasha caught up with him and shoved him in the back, and the boy fell headlong. The gardener seized him a second time and secured him with his belt.

"Give me the ring!" Sasha shouted.

"Wait a moment, young master," said Stepan. "We'll take him to the steward—he'll know what to do with him."

The gardener led the prisoner to the main courtyard, and Sasha went with them, looking anxiously now and again at his trousers, which were torn and grass-stained. Suddenly all three found themselves face to face with Kirila Petrovich, who was on his way to inspect the stables.

"What's going on?" he asked Stepan.

Stepan quickly outlined what he had seen. Kirila Petrovich listened attentively.

"Little rascal," he said, turning to Sasha, "what were you fighting about?"

"He stole the ring from the hollow oak, Papenka. Tell him to give back the ring!"

"What ring? What hollow oak?"

"The one Maria Kirilovna...The ring..."

Sasha stammered in confusion. Kirila Petrovich frowned and shook his head. "So Maria Kirilovna's mixed up in all this, is she? You'd better make a clean breast of it now—or I'll thrash you within an inch of your life."

"I swear, Papenka, I...Papenka...Maria Kirilovna didn't ask me to do anything, Papenka."

"Stepan, go and cut me a birch switch, a nice young one."

"Wait, Papenka, I'll tell you everything. I was running about in the yard, and my sister opened the window, and I ran there, and Maria Kirilovna threw down the ring accidentally, and I hid it in the hollow oak, and . . . and . . . this red-headed boy tried to steal the ring . . ."

"Threw down the ring accidentally—and you tried to hide it . . . Stepan, get me some switches."

"Wait, Papenka, let me tell you everything. My sister Maria Kirilovna told me to run down to the oak and put the ring in the hollow, but this horrid boy . . ."

Kirila Petrovich turned to the horrid boy and asked sternly, "Where are you from?"

"I am a house serf of the Dubrovsky family," answered the red-headed boy.

Kirila Petrovich's face darkened.

"It seems you don't acknowledge me as your master—very well. And what were you doing in my garden?"

"Stealing raspberries," the boy answered, with great equanimity.

"Ah, I see! Like master, like man—judge the flock by its priest. And do raspberries really grow on my oak trees?"

The boy said nothing.

"Papenka, tell him to give me back the ring," said Sasha.

"Quiet, Sasha," said Kirila Petrovich, "and remember—I haven't finished with you yet. Go to your room. And you, squint-eyes, you seem like a bright lad. Give back the ring and be off with you."

The boy opened his fist and showed there was nothing in it.

"If you tell me everything, I won't thrash you. I'll even give you five kopeks so you can buy yourself some nuts. But if you don't, you'll get more than you've bargained for. Well?"

The boy said nothing. He hung his head and looked as if he were a half-wit.

"Very well," said Kirila Petrovich, "lock him up somewhere and make sure he doesn't get out—or I'll skin the lot of you."

Stepan took the boy to the dovecot, locked him up there, and told Agafya, the old poultry woman, to keep watch on him.

"We must send for the police captain," said Kirila Petrovich, still watching the boy, "and as quickly as possible."

"No doubt about it," thought Kirila Petrovich, "she's kept up with that accursed Dubrovsky. But has she really been appealing to him for help?" He was pacing about the room, furiously whistling "Thunder of Victory, Resound!" "Maybe, after all this time, I'm hot on his heels! Yes, he won't slip away from us now. We must seize the opportunity. Ha! A bell! The Lord be praised—it's the police captain... Hey, fetch that little brat we've just captured."

A cart had driven into the yard. Our old acquaintance the police captain, covered in dust, entered the room.

"Splendid news," said Kirila Petrovich. "I've caught Dubrovsky."

"The Lord be praised, Your Excellency!" said the delighted police captain. "Where is he?"

"That is, not Dubrovsky himself, but one of his gang. They're bringing him in. He'll help us to capture the chieftain. Here he is."

The police captain, expecting a fearsome brigand, was amazed to see a rather puny-looking thirteen-year-old boy. He turned to Kirila Petrovich in bewilderment, waiting for an explanation. Kirila Petrovich then related the events of the morning, without, however, mentioning Maria Kirilovna.

The police captain listened attentively, glancing frequently at the boy; the little rascal was pretending to be an idiot and seemed to be paying no attention at all to anything going on around him.

"Allow me, Your Excellency, to have a word with you in private," said the police captain finally.

Kirila Petrovich took him to another room and locked the door.

Half an hour later they returned to the hall, where the prisoner was waiting for his fate to be decided.

"The master wanted to have you locked up in the town jail, given a good thrashing, and sent to Siberia," said the police captain, "but I interceded on your behalf and won you a pardon... Untie him!"

The boy was untied.

"Thank your master," said the police captain. The boy went up to Kirila Petrovich and kissed his hand.

"You go home now," said Kirila Petrovich, "and don't go stealing any more raspberries from hollow oaks."

The boy went out, jumped joyfully down the front steps, and, without looking back, dashed off across the fields to Kisteniovka. When he got there, he stopped at a little tumbledown hut, at the very edge of the village, and knocked at the window; the window opened, and an old woman looked out.

"Give me some bread, Granny," said the boy. "I've had nothing to eat since breakfast, I'm starving."

"Ah, it's you, Mitya. But where've you been all day, you little devil?" said the old woman.

"I'll tell you later, granny. For the love of God, give me some bread!"

"Come inside then."

"I haven't got time, Granny. I have to go somewhere, I'm in a hurry. Bread—give me some bread, for the love of Christ!"

"All right, you little madcap, here you are!" the old woman muttered, and thrust a piece of black bread through the window. The boy greedily bit into it and rushed off, still chewing.

It was beginning to grow dark. Mitya made his way past barns and vegetable plots to the Kisteniovka wood. When he came to two pine trees standing like sentinels at the edge of the wood, he stopped, looked carefully all round, let out a shrill staccato whistle, then stood and listened; there was a long, soft answering whistle and someone came out of the wood towards him.

18

Kirila Petrovich was walking up and down the hall, whistling his tune more loudly than ever; the entire house was in commotion, servants were running backwards and forwards, maids were bustling about, coachmen were preparing the carriage, and the yard was crowded with people. Maria Kirilovna was in her dressing room; a lady surrounded by servants was standing in front of a mirror and attending to her attire. Maria was pale and motionless, her head drooping languidly under the weight of her diamonds; sometimes she gave a slight start when pricked by a careless hand, but she said nothing, gazing vacantly into the mirror.

"Are you nearly ready?" Kirila Petrovich called from just outside.

"In a moment," replied the lady. "Maria Kirilovna, stand up and look at yourself. Is everything in order?"

Maria Kirilovna got to her feet and said nothing. The door opened.

"The bride is ready," the lady said to Kirila Petrovich. "Tell her to take her place in the carriage."

"With God's blessing," Kirila Petrovich replied, taking an icon from the table. "Come here, Masha," he said to her with emotion, "let me give you my blessing." The poor girl fell at his feet and burst out sobbing.

"Papenka, Papenka…" she said through her tears, and her voice failed her. Kirila Petrovich hurriedly blessed her. She was helped to her feet and almost carried out to the carriage. The matron of honor[31] and a maidservant got in with her. They drove to the church. The groom was already waiting. He came out to greet the bride and was struck by her pallor and strange look. Together they entered the cold, empty church; the doors were locked behind them. The priest came out from behind the iconostasis and immediately began. Maria Kirilovna saw nothing, heard nothing, and could think of only one thing; she had been waiting for Dubrovsky since early that morning. Not for one moment had hope left her, but when the priest turned to her with the customary questions, she shuddered and went faint. Yet she remained silent, still waiting. The priest, hearing no answer from her, pronounced the irrevocable words.

The ceremony was over. She felt the cold kiss of a husband she did not love and heard joyful words of congratulation. She was still unable to believe that her life had been fettered forever and that Dubrovsky had not rushed to her rescue. The prince turned to her with tender words that she did not understand. They left the church; the porch was crowded with peasants from Pokrovskoye. She ran her gaze quickly over them and slipped back into her former apathy. Bride and groom got into the carriage together and set off for Arbatovo; Kirila Petrovich had gone on ahead to greet them on their arrival. Alone with his young wife, the prince was not in the least troubled by her cold manner. He did not irritate her with cloying protestations and absurd raptures;

his words were simple and required no reply. So they drove for about seven miles, the horses going at a fast trot over the bumps of the country road and the carriage barely swaying on its English springs. Suddenly they heard shouting, the carriage stopped, a crowd of armed men surrounded it, and a man in a half-mask, opening the door beside the young princess, said to her, "You are free. Get down." "What's all this?" shouted the prince, "and who are you?" "It's Dubrovsky," said the princess. The prince, not losing his presence of mind, took a traveling pistol from a side pocket and shot at the masked brigand. The princess shrieked in horror and covered her face with her hands. Dubrovsky was wounded in the shoulder; he was bleeding. The prince immediately took out another pistol, but he was given no time to use it; the door on his side opened, and several strong hands dragged him out of the carriage and snatched the pistol away. Knives flashed above him.

"Don't touch him!" shouted Dubrovsky, and his grim comrades drew back.

"You are free," Dubrovsky repeated, turning to the pale princess.

"No," she answered. "It's too late. I am married, I am the wife of Prince Vereisky."

"What are you saying?" Dubrovsky cried out in despair. "No, you are not his wife, you were coerced, you could never have given your consent."

"I consented, I made a vow," she replied firmly. "The prince is my husband. Tell your men to let him go, and leave me with him. I did not deceive you. I waited for you until the last minute. But now, I tell you—now it is too late. Release us."

But Dubrovsky could no longer hear her: the pain from his wound and the turbulence in his soul had taken away his strength. He collapsed beside one of the carriage wheels, and his men gathered around him. He managed to say a few words, and they put him on his horse. Two of them supported him, a third led the horse by the bridle, and they went off across the fields, leaving the carriage in the middle of the road, the servants bound, and the horses unharnessed; but they had neither stolen anything nor shed a single drop of blood in revenge for their chief's blood.

19

In a narrow clearing deep in the forest was a small stronghold consisting of a ditch and a rampart, behind which were a few huts and dugouts.

A number of men, immediately identifiable as brigands from their motley dress and the fact that they all bore arms, were eating their dinner there, sitting around a communal cauldron. A sentry was sitting on the rampart beside a small cannon, his legs tucked under him; he was sewing a patch onto one of his garments, plying his needle with the skill of an experienced tailor while repeatedly looking about him in every direction.

Although a cup had been passed around several times, a strange silence reigned over the gathering. The brigands finished their dinner and, one after another, got to their feet and said their prayers; some went to their huts while others wandered off into the forest or lay down for a brief nap.

The sentry finished his sewing, shook out the tattered garment, admired the patch, stuck the needle into his sleeve, and burst out, at the top of his voice, into an old melancholy song:

> Green mother, green dubrovka,[32] don't rustle,
> Don't stop a young lad from dreaming his dreams.

The door of one of the huts opened and an old woman appeared on the threshold. She had a white cap on her head and was neatly dressed. "Enough of that, Stepka," she said angrily. "The master's resting—and you have to start bawling. Are you all without conscience or pity?" "I beg pardon, Yegorovna," Stepka answered. "Don't worry, I'll be quiet now. Let the young master sleep and get his strength back!" The old woman went back into the hut, and Stepka began pacing about the rampart.

Inside the hut, lying on a camp bed behind a partition, was the wounded Dubrovsky. His pistols were on a small table beside him, and his sword was hanging at the head of the bed. The floor and walls of the mud hut were covered by rich rugs, and in one corner stood a lady's silvered dressing table and mirror. Dubrovsky had an open book in his hand, but his eyes were closed. The old woman, who kept peeping round from the other side of the partition, could not be sure whether he was asleep or merely lost in thought.

Suddenly Dubrovsky started; an alarm sounded inside the stronghold, and Stepka thrust his head through the window. "Vladimir Andreyevich, sir!" he shouted. "They're on our track! Our men have just signaled." Dubrovsky leaped out of bed, seized his weapons, and went outside. The brigands, who had been milling about noisily, fell silent. "Are you all here?" asked Dubrovsky. "All except the scouts," came the answer. "To your positions!" Dubrovsky shouted, and each man went to his place. Three scouts came running towards the gates. Dubrovsky went to meet them. "What's happening?" he asked. "There are soldiers in the wood," they replied. "We're being surrounded." Dubrovsky ordered the gate to be locked and went over to check the small cannon. There were voices in the wood; they were coming closer. The brigands waited in silence. Three or four soldiers appeared from among the trees and at once drew back, firing shots as a signal to their comrades. "Prepare for battle!" said Dubrovsky. There was a murmur from among the brigands, then everything went silent. They heard the noise of approaching soldiers; weapons glinted from between the trees, and around a hundred and fifty men poured out of the wood and rushed shouting towards the rampart. Dubrovsky lit the fuse; the cannon fired; one soldier had his head torn off and two were wounded. The soldiers were thrown into confusion but their officer dashed forward and the soldiers followed, rushing into the ditch; the brigands shot at them with guns and pistols and then waited, holding their axes ready: the frenzied soldiers, having left around twenty wounded comrades in the ditch below, were now trying to climb the rampart. There was a hand-to-hand struggle. The soldiers had reached the top of the rampart and the brigands were beginning to lose ground, but Dubrovsky went up close to the officer, put his pistol to his chest and fired; the man fell backwards. A group of soldiers picked him up in their arms and quickly carried him away; the others, having lost their leader, stopped. Emboldened, the brigands took advantage of this moment of confusion, pressing the soldiers back and forcing them down into the ditch. The soldiers took flight and the brigands chased after them, yelling and shrieking. The battle was won. Confident that the enemy were now routed, Dubrovsky called his men off. He then gave orders to bring in the wounded and shut himself away in his stronghold, doubling the number of sentries and forbidding anyone to leave.

After this battle the government began to pay more serious attention to Dubrovsky's daring robberies. Intelligence about the places he frequented was gathered. A detachment of soldiers was sent out, ordered to capture him dead or alive. A few members of his band were caught, and it was learned that Dubrovsky was no longer among them. A few days after the battle he had gathered together his companions, announced that he was leaving them for good, and advised them to change their way of life. "You have grown rich under my command, and each of you has a pass with which you can make your way to some distant province and live there for the rest of your life, working honestly and prosperously. But you're all rascals and you probably won't want to give up your present trade." After this he left them, taking with him only one man. No one knew what had become of him. At first the authorities doubted this testimony; the brigands' devotion to their chief was well known. It was supposed that they were trying to shield him. Subsequent events, however, confirmed that the brigands had spoken the truth: the raids, fires, and robberies came to an end. The roads became safe. From other reports it was learned that Dubrovsky had escaped abroad.

Translated by Robert and Elizabeth Chandler

THE EGYPTIAN NIGHTS

—*Quel est cet homme?*
—*Ha! C'est un bien grand talent, il fait de sa voix tout ce qu'il veut.*
—*Il devrait bien, madame, s'en faire une culotte.*[1]

I

CHARSKY was a native citizen of Petersburg. He was not yet thirty; he was unmarried; his work in the civil service was not burdensome. His late uncle, a vice-governor during prosperous times, had left him a decent estate. His life could have been most pleasant; but he had the misfortune to write and publish poetry. In journals he was called a poet; in servants' quarters a scribbler.

For all the great advantages enjoyed by versifiers—although, apart from the right to use the accusative instead of the genitive and a few other examples of so-called poetic license, we know of no particular advantages enjoyed by Russian versifiers ... But be that as it may—in spite of all possible advantages, these people are also subject to great disadvantages and unpleasantnesses. The versifier's bitterest, most unbearable affliction is his title, his sobriquet, with which he is branded and from which he can never escape. The public look on him as their property; in their opinion, he is born for their benefit and pleasure. Should he return from the country, the first person he meets will greet him with, "Haven't you brought anything new for us?" Should he be deep in thought about the disorder of his affairs, or with regard to the illness of someone close to him, a trite smile will at once accompany the trite exclamation: "No doubt you're composing something?" Should he fall in love, his beauty will buy herself an album from the English Shop and expect him to compose elegies. If he goes to visit someone he hardly knows, to talk about an important matter, the man will summon his son and make him read *this gentleman's* poems aloud—and the little boy will treat the versifier to the versifier's own, mangled, poems. And if these are the laurels of the craft, then imagine its pains! The greetings, requests, albums, and little boys were so very irritating, Charsky confessed, that he had to be constantly on his guard lest he let slip some offensive remark.

Charsky made every possible effort to escape the insufferable sobriquet. He avoided his fellow men of letters, preferring the company of even the most vacuous members of high society. His conversation was exceedingly banal and never touched on literature. In his dress he always followed the latest fashion with the diffidence and superstition of a young Muscovite visiting Petersburg for the very first time. His study, furnished like a lady's bedroom, did not in any respect call to mind that of a writer; no books were piled on or under the tables; the sofa was not stained with ink; there was none of the disorder that reveals the presence of the Muse and the absence of dustpan and brush. Charsky despaired if one of his society friends discovered him pen in hand. It is hard to believe that a man endowed with talent and a soul could stoop to such petty dissimulation. He would pretend to be a passionate lover of horses, a desperate gambler, or the most discriminating of gourmets—even though he could not tell a mountain pony from an Arab steed, could never remember trumps, and secretly preferred baked potatoes to every possible invention of French cuisine. He led the most distracted of lives; he was present at every ball, he ate too much at every diplomatic dinner, and at every reception he was as inevitable as Rezanov's ice cream.

But he was a poet, and his passion was not to be overcome. When he sensed the approach of that *nonsense* (his word for inspiration), Charsky would lock himself in his study and write from morning till late at night. Only then, he would confess to his closest friends, did he know true happiness. The rest of the time he went out and about, put on airs, dissembled, and was subjected again and again to the glorious question, "Have you written anything new?"

One morning, Charsky was in that state of grace when fancies outline themselves clearly before you and you discover vivid, unexpected words to embody your visions, when verses flow readily from your pen and resonant rhymes come forward to meet orderly thoughts. He was plunged in sweet forgetfulness—and society, society's opinions, and his own foibles no longer existed for him. He was writing poetry.

Suddenly his study door creaked and he saw the head of a stranger. He started and frowned.

"Who's that?" he asked in annoyance, mentally cursing his servants for always leaving his vestibule unattended.

The stranger entered.

He was tall and lean, and he looked about thirty. The features of his swarthy face were distinctive: a pale, high forehead shaded by dark locks, gleaming black eyes, an aquiline nose, and a thick beard framing sunken, bronzed cheeks—all these made it clear he was a foreigner. He was wearing a black frock coat, turning white along the seams, and summer trousers (even though it was now well into autumn), and on his yellowish shirt front, beneath a worn black cravat, shone a false diamond; his fraying hat had clearly seen both sun and rain. Meeting this man in a forest, you'd take him for a brigand; in society—for a political conspirator; in your vestibule—for a charlatan peddling elixirs and rat poison.

"What do you want?" Charsky asked, in French.

"Signore," the foreigner answered with low bows, "*Lei voglia perdonarmi se...*"[2]

Rather than offering him a chair, Charsky got to his feet. The conversation continued in Italian.

"I am a Neapolitan artist," said the stranger. "Circumstances have obliged me to leave my homeland. Trusting in my talent, I have come to Russia."

Charsky thought the Neapolitan intended to give some cello recitals and was selling tickets from door to door. He was about to hand the man his twenty-five rubles, to get rid of him quickly, but the stranger went on, "I hope, Signore, that you will be able to assist a fellow artist and introduce me to the houses where you yourself are received."

No blow to Charsky's vanity could have been sharper. He looked haughtily at the man who called himself his fellow artist. "Allow me to ask who I am speaking to and who you take me to be," he said, struggling to hold back his indignation.

The Neapolitan sensed Charsky's annoyance.

"Signore," he stammered, "*ho creduto . . . ho sentito . . . la Vostra Eccellenza mi perdonerà . . .*"[3]

"What do you want?" Charsky asked drily.

"I have heard a great deal about your astonishing talent; I am certain that gentlemen here consider it an honor to offer their patronage in every possible way to so outstanding a poet," the Italian replied, "and I have therefore taken the liberty of presenting myself to you—"

"You are mistaken, Signore," Charsky interrupted. "The title of poet does not exist here. Our poets do not enjoy the patronage of gentlemen; our poets are themselves gentlemen, and if our Maecenases (the devil take them!) don't know this, then so much the worse for them. Here we have no tattered abbés whom a composer might take off the street to write a libretto. Our poets don't go on foot from door to door, soliciting donations—and all they ask from Maecenases (the devil take them!) is that they should not secretly denounce them (and not even this wish is granted).[4] And whoever told you I am a great versifier must have been jesting. I admit I did once write a few poor epigrams, but, thank God, I neither have, nor wish to have, anything to do with gentlemen versifiers."

The poor Italian was in confusion. He glanced round the room. The paintings, the marble statues and bronze busts, the expensive gewgaws displayed on Gothic étagères, astonished him. He understood that there was nothing in common between himself, a poor wandering artiste in a worn cravat and an old frock coat, and this haughty dandy standing before him in a tufted brocade skullcap and a gold-embroidered Chinese gown with a Turkish shawl for a belt. He uttered some incoherent excuses, bowed, and was about to leave. His pathetic look moved Charsky, who, for all his affectations, had a kind and noble heart. He felt ashamed of being so quick to take offense.

"Where are you going?" he said to the Italian. "Wait. I had to decline an undeserved title and confess to you that I am no poet. Now let us talk about your own affairs. I am ready to be of service to you in any way I can. You are a musician?"

"No, Eccellenza!" the Italian answered. "I am a poor improvvisatore."

"An improvvisatore!" exclaimed Charsky, sensing all the cruelty of his behavior. "Why didn't you say at once that you're an improvvisatore?" And Charsky pressed the Italian's hand with a sense of genuine remorse.

His friendly air was reassuring. Straightforwardly, the Italian began to deliver himself of his proposal. His outward appearance was not deceptive. He needed money; he was hoping, here in Russia, to get his personal affairs onto a sounder footing. Charsky listened to him attentively.

"I hope," he said to the poor artist, "that you will enjoy success; society here has never heard an improvvisatore before. Curiosity will be aroused. Italian, I admit, is not spoken here, so you will not be understood, but that doesn't matter. What matters is that you should be in vogue."

"But if no one here understands Italian," said the improvvisatore after a little thought, "who will come and listen to me?"

"They will come, don't worry—some out of curiosity, some for a way of passing the evening, and others to show that they understand Italian. What matters, I repeat, is that you should be in vogue—and you will be in vogue, you have my word for it."

After noting his address, Charsky parted affectionately with the improvvisatore, and that very evening he began making arrangements on his behalf.

2

I'm Tsar and slave, I'm worm and God.

—GAVRILA DERZHAVIN, "God"

THE FOLLOWING day Charsky was walking down a dark, dirty tavern corridor looking for room 35. He stopped at the door and knocked. Yesterday's Italian opened it.

"Victory!" said Charsky. "Everything's as good as done. The Princess —— is lending you her hall. At a reception last night I managed to recruit half of Petersburg—you must print your tickets and announcements. I guarantee you, if not a triumph, at least some profit."

"That's what matters!" exclaimed the Italian, showing his joy through the lively gestures of a man from the south. "I knew you would help me. *Corpo di Bacco!*[5] You're a poet, just as I am; and say what you like, poets are splendid fellows! How can I express my gratitude? Wait...would you like to hear an improvisation?"

"An improvisation! But surely you need an audience, and music, and the thunder of applause?"

"Nonsense, nonsense! Where can I find a better audience? You are a poet, you will understand me better than anyone, and your quiet encouragement means more to me than a whole storm of applause... Find somewhere to sit and give me a theme."

Charsky sat down on a trunk (one of the two chairs in the cramped little kennel was broken, the other covered by a heap of papers and linen). The improvvisatore took a guitar from the table—and stood facing Charsky, plucking the strings with bony fingers and waiting for his command.

"Here's a theme for you," said Charsky. "'It is for the poet to choose the matter of his songs himself; the crowd has no right to direct his inspiration.'"

The Italian's eyes gleamed; he played a few chords, proudly flung back his head—and impassioned verses, the expression of immediate feeling, flew harmoniously from his lips. Here they are, freely transcribed by one of our friends from the words preserved in Charsky's memory:

> Here comes the poet—he can see
> No one, and yet he's open-eyed.
> Then someone's pulling at his sleeve
> And he must listen while they chide:
> "No sooner have you climbed to heaven
> Than back to earth you cast your eyes;
> By what strange power are you driven
> To wander down such aimless ways?
> A fruitless fever grips your soul;
> Your vision's blurred, your view's obscured;
> It seems you can't escape the hold
> Of matters pointless and absurd.
> A genius soars above the earthly;
> True poets sense an obligation
> Only to sing what's truly worthy
> The Muses and their inspiration."
> What makes the wind sweep down ravines
> And whirl dry leaves through dusty air,
> While ships becalmed on silent seas
> Wait for its kiss in blank despair?
> What makes the eagle leave his height
> And, flying past towers, choose to alight
> On some old stump? The eagle knows.
> And Desdemona's heart is closed
> To all but black Othello, whom
> She loves—just as the moon adores
> The blackest night. Hearts know no laws;

Eagles and winds are free to roam.
A poet too is like the wind;
He too escapes all ties that bind.
And like the eagle, he flies far;
Like Desdemona, he must love
Whatever idol charms his heart,
And not care who may disapprove.

The Italian fell silent. Charsky said nothing, amazed and moved.

"Well?" the improvvisatore repeated.

Charsky took his hand and pressed it firmly.

"Well?" the improvvisatore repeated. "What do you think?"

"Astonishing!" said the poet. "How can this be? Another person's thought has barely reached your ears—and at once you make it your own, as if you've been nursing it, cherishing it, tirelessly developing it. For you, then, there exists neither labor, nor dejection, nor the anxiety that precedes inspiration. Astonishing, quite astonishing!"

The improvvisatore answered, "Every talent is inexplicable. How is it that a sculptor, seeing a slab of Carrara marble, can glimpse a hidden Jupiter and bring him out into the light, splitting the stone casing with hammer and chisel? Why does a thought leave a poet's head already equipped with four rhymes and divided into feet that are harmonious and of equal length? Similarly, no one but the improvvisatore himself can understand this quickness of impressions, this intimate link between his own inspiration and the will of a stranger. Even my own attempts to explain this would be in vain. However... it's time to think about my first evening. What do you suggest? How should tickets be priced so as neither to burden the public nor leave me out of pocket? *La signora* Catalani,[6] they say, charged twenty-five roubles. That's not a bad price."

Charsky found it unpleasant to be brought down so suddenly from the heights of poetry to the bookkeeper's office; but he well understood the imperatives of everyday need, and, together with the Italian, he plunged into matters pecuniary. The Italian then revealed such unbridled greed, such an unabashed love of profit, that Charsky felt truly disgusted. He hastened to leave, so as not to lose entirely the sense of wonder the brilliant improvvisatore had aroused in him. The preoccupied Italian did not notice this change; he accompanied Charsky along the corridor and down the staircase, seeing him off with deep bows and assurances of eternal gratitude.

3

Tickets are ten rubles each; the
performance begins at 7 p.m.

—A poster

THE PRINCESS'S reception hall had been placed at the improvvisatore's disposal. A stage had been erected and chairs set out in twelve rows; on the appointed day, by seven o'clock, the hall was lit up and an old long-nosed woman, wearing a gray hat with broken feathers and with rings on all her fingers, was sitting at a little table by the door, checking and selling tickets. Gendarmes stood by the main entrance. The audience began to gather. Charsky was among the first to arrive. He was very concerned that the performance should be a success, and he wanted to see the improvvisatore and find out if everything was to his liking. He found the Italian in a little side room, glancing impatiently at his watch. The Italian was dressed theatrically—in black from head to toe. The lace collar of his shirt was turned back, the strange whiteness of his bare neck stood out sharply against his thick black beard, and locks of hair hung down over his forehead and eyebrows. Charsky greatly disliked all this, finding it unpleasant to see a poet in the costume of a traveling player. After exchanging a few words, he returned to the hall, which was filling up steadily.

Soon the chairs were all occupied by dazzling ladies; tightly framing the ladies, the men stood in front of the stage, along the walls, and behind the last row of chairs. The musicians and their music stands took up both sides of the stage. On a table in the middle stood a porcelain vase. There were a lot of people, all waiting impatiently.

At half past seven the musicians finally bestirred themselves; they raised their bows and began the overture to *Tancredi*.[7] After the last notes of the overture had thundered out, everything went still and silent. And the improvvisatore, greeted by deafening applause from all sides, advanced with low bows to the very edge of the stage.

Charsky had been feeling anxious, wondering what impression the first minute would make, but he noticed that the Italian's costume, which to him had seemed so unfortunate, appeared otherwise to the audience. Charsky himself found nothing absurd in the man when he saw him on stage, his pallid face brightly lit by a multitude of candles and lamps. The applause died away; conversation ceased. The Italian, speaking in broken French, asked the ladies and gentlemen present to jot down some themes, writing them on separate bits of paper. At this unexpected invitation, the audience all began looking at one another in silence; no one responded. The Italian waited a little, then repeated his request in a timid and deferential voice. Charsky was standing right by the stage; he was seized with anxiety, sensing that nothing would happen without him and that he would have to write down a theme himself. Several women's heads had indeed turned towards him and begun to call out his name, at first softly, then louder and louder. Hearing this, the improvvisatore looked round for Charsky, saw him there at his feet, and, with a friendly smile, handed him pencil and paper. Charsky found it most unpleasant to have to play a role in this comedy, but he had no choice: he took the pencil and paper from the Italian's hands and wrote a few words; the Italian took the vase from the table, stepped down from the stage, and held the vase out to Charsky, who dropped in his piece of paper. This set an effective example: two journalists considered it their duty as men of letters to write down a theme each; the secretary of the Neapolitan embassy and some young man, only recently returned from his travels and still raving about Florence, placed their folded papers in the urn; lastly, at her mother's bidding, a plain young girl with tears in her eyes wrote a few lines in Italian and, blushing to her ears, handed them to the improvvisatore; the ladies watched in silence, with faint smiles of mockery. Returning to his stage, the improvvisatore put the urn back on the table and began, one by one, to take out the pieces of paper, reading each of them aloud:

> The Cenci family (*La famiglia dei Cenci*).
> *L'ultimo giorno di Pompeia.*
> *Cleopatra e i suoi amanti.*
> *La primavera veduta da una prigione.*
> *Il trionfo di Tasso.*[8]

"What is the wish of the esteemed company?" asked the deferential Italian. "Will you yourselves select one of the proposed themes, or will you let the matter be decided by lot?"

"By lot!" said a voice from the crowd.

"By lot, by lot!" the audience repeated.

The improvvisatore stepped down again from the stage, holding the urn in his hands, and asked, "Who will be so kind as to draw a theme?" He looked entreatingly up and down the front rows. Not one of the dazzling ladies moved a finger. The improvvisatore, unaccustomed to northern indifference, seemed agitated. Then, over to one side, he noticed a raised hand, in a small white glove; he quickly turned round and walked up to a majestic young beauty sitting at the end of the second row. She stood up without any embarrassment and, with the utmost simplicity, put her small aristocratic hand into the urn and drew out a folded slip of paper.

"Be so kind as to unfold the paper and read it out," said the improvvisatore. The beauty unfolded the paper and read aloud: "*Cleopatra e i suoi amanti.*"

These words were pronounced quietly, but such was the silence reigning over the hall that everyone heard them. The improvvisatore bowed, with an air of deep gratitude, to the beautiful lady and returned to his stage.

"Ladies and gentlemen," he said, turning to the audience, "the lot proposes I improvise on the theme of Cleopatra and her lovers. I humbly ask whoever chose this theme to clarify their thought: which lovers did they have in mind—*perché la grande regina n'aveva molti?*"[9]

At these words many of the men burst into loud laughter. The improvvisatore appeared somewhat confused.

"I should like to know," he went on, "which historical moment was in the mind of the person who proposed this theme . . . I shall be most grateful if they can clarify this."

No one responded. Several ladies glanced at the plain young girl who had written down a theme at her mother's bidding. The poor girl noticed this unkind attention and was in such confusion that tears appeared on her eyelashes. Charsky could not bear this and, turning to the improvvisatore, said to him in Italian, "It was I who suggested the theme. I had in mind the testimony of, who maintains that Cleopatra proposed death as the price for her love, and that there were admirers neither frightened nor repelled by this condition. I think, however, that the subject is a little difficult. Perhaps you would prefer to choose another?"

But the improvvisatore could already sense the approach of the god. He signaled to the musicians to play. His face went terribly pale and he began to tremble as if from fever; his eyes gleamed with a strange fire; he smoothed back his black hair with one hand and, with a handkerchief, wiped beads of sweat from his high forehead. Suddenly he strode forward, folding his arms across his chest. The music died away. The improvisation began.

> The palace shines. Sweet melodies,
> Accompanied by flute and lyre,
> And her sweet voice, and her bright eyes,
> Make light of dark, make night expire.
> All hearts bow down towards her throne;
> She is the Queen whom all must court—
> But then her own fair head sinks down
> Towards her golden cup in thought.
>
> Flutes, lyres, and voices—all goes dead.
> A deepening silence fills the hall.
> But when once more she lifts her head,

Her words both frighten and enthrall:
"My love holds bliss, so I keep hearing.
If there is truth in what you claim,
Blessed is he whose love has daring
Enough to pay the price I name.
My contract binds all equally:
He who would claim me as his wife,
He who desires one night with me,
Must for that night lay down his life.

"Once I lie on the bed of pleasure—
I swear by all the gods above—
I'll bring delight beyond all measure
Yet be the humblest slave of love.
Hear me, O splendid Aphrodite,
And you, dread god who reigns below,
And you above, great Zeus almighty—
I swear: until the dawn's first glow
Brightens the sky, I shall divine
Each hidden wish of my lord's heart;
I'll set on fire, then soothe with wine;
I'll bare the mysteries of love's art.
But when the eastern sky turns red,
When my lord feels the morning's breath,
Soldiers will lead him from my bed
To meet the lasting kiss of death."

All hearts rebel, and yet they all
Remain enslaved by beauty's charm.
Uncertain murmurs fill the hall;
She listens with untroubled calm
And looks around with haughty pride,
Thinking her suitors spurn her offer.
Then one emerges from the crowd;
Two others follow quickly after.

Their steps are bold, their eyes are bright;
She rises to her feet to meet them.
The bargain's struck; each buys one night,
And when it's over, death will greet them.

The lovers' lots are blessed by priests
And dropped inside the fateful urn.
Then, watched in silence by the guests,
A lot is drawn. First comes the turn,
The gods decree, of gallant Flavius,
Flavius whose courage never wavers.
Such scorn in a mere woman's eyes
Is more than Flavius can endure;
Amazed by Cleopatra's gall,
This gray-haired veteran of war
Now leaps to answer pleasure's call
As once he answered battle cries.
Criton comes next, a youthful sage
Born in the groves of Epicure,
Whose graceful verses sing the rage
Induced by Venus and Amor.
The third is like a glowing rose
Whose petals dawn has coaxed apart,
A joy to both the eye and heart,
A youth whose name the centuries
Have lost. The softest shadow lies
Over his cheeks; love fills his eyes.
The passions raging in his breast
Are like a still-closed book to him
And Cleopatra looks at him
With eyes surprised by tenderness.

Translated by Robert and Elizabeth Chandler

AFTERWORD

I

THE NEVER-completed *Peter the Great's African* was Pushkin's first serious attempt at a novel. He himself always referred to it simply as "a historical novel." It was given its title by his editors, when they first published it in 1837, soon after Pushkin's death.

From his student days Pushkin had been deeply interested in Russian history. In 1831 he was appointed Russia's official historian laureate (*istoriograf*). He was only the second person—after the poet and historian Nikolay Karamzin—to be given this title, and he took it as a great honor; he was well aware that Voltaire, whom he admired, had been granted a similar title by Louis XV. Pushkin made use of this position to do serious, detailed archival research, both for his completed *History of Pugachov* and for his unfinished study of Peter the Great.

One of Pushkin's most eloquent statements about Russian history is in a letter he wrote to the philosopher Pyotr Chaadaev, expressing his disagreement with Chaadaev's argument—laid out in the first of his *Philosophical Letters*—that Russia somehow stands outside history, that it has no history worth the name. Russia, Pushkin retorted, had its own special mission, an important part of which had been to absorb the Mongol conquest. Pushkin goes on to mention other significant moments in Russian history, and such figures as "Peter the Great, who in himself alone is a universal history! And Catherine II, who placed Russia on the threshold of Europe. And Alexander, who led us to Paris." He concludes, "Not for anything in the world would I be willing to change my fatherland, nor to have any other history than that of our ancestors, such as God gave it to us."[1]

Pushkin lends added weight to this assertion by dating his letter "19 October 1836"—the same date that he gave for completing *The Captain's Daughter*. Pushkin had entered the Imperial Lycée twenty-five years earlier, on 19 October 1811, and he had written several important poems on anniversaries of this date. It was a date intimately linked for him with reflections on his own fate, the fate of his contemporaries—several of whom had been hanged or exiled for their part in the Decembrist Revolt of 1825—and the fate of Russia itself. It was, in effect, a variant of his signature, reserved for matters of heartfelt importance.

As the letter suggests, the historical figure who most fascinated Pushkin was Peter the Great. Peter plays a central role in several of Pushkin's works: not only *Peter the Great's African* and the unfinished historical study, but also two of his narrative poems, *Poltava* and *The Bronze Horseman*. One reason why Pushkin kept returning to this theme may have been the difficulty he encountered in finding a vantage point that would grant him a clear view of Peter the Great. In the summer of 1833, Pushkin said to the lexicographer Vladimir Dal', "Up to now I still cannot understand and comprehend intellectually that giant: he is too huge for us short-sighted ones, and we are still too close to him—one has to move away two centuries—but I understand him emotionally; the longer I study him, the more astonishment and reverence deprive me of the means of thinking and judging freely."[2] Svetlana Evdokimova suggests that Pushkin tried to resolve this difficulty by studying Peter from a variety of perspectives, through the prisms of different literary genres.[3] In *Poltava* he presents Peter as a warrior-hero, defeating the Swedish Empire and so ensuring Russia's survival as a European power. In *The Bronze Horseman* he shows us Peter's towering figure continuing to oppress ordinary Russians, even a century after his death. And in *Peter the Great's African* we see how Peter's sweeping reforms affected Russian society at the time, how they shaped the lives of people of different social classes. It is this that was Pushkin's concern; he makes no attempt to enter into Peter's consciousness, to understand what he thought and felt.

The Pushkins belonged to the old Russian nobility. Pushkin was proud of this and many of his works allude to episodes from his family's past. His ancestor Afanasy Pushkin, for example, plays a minor role in the historical drama *Boris Godunov*, and Pushkin lends some aspects of his family history both to the Dubrovskys and to the Grinyov family in *The Captain's Daughter*. It is hardly surprising, then, that Pushkin should give a central role in a novel about Peter the Great to his maternal great-grandfather, Abram Gannibal. Not only was Gannibal a close confidant of Peter's, but he was also a figure of considerable interest in his own right. The surname he chose for himself (Gannibal is the standard Russian transliteration of Hannibal) shows that he was aware of his importance and unabashed about asserting it.

Probably born around 1696–98 near Lake Chad, in what is now Cameroon, Gannibal may have been the son of a minor prince. He was abducted as a child and sold as a slave in Constantinople. He was then purchased by the Russian ambassador to the Ottoman Empire and presented as a gift to Peter the Great; he was then probably about eight. Peter appears to have been quick to notice the boy's unusual intelligence, adopting him as his godson and giving him the best possible education. He was soon taking him on military campaigns as his valet.

Gannibal proved equally gifted in languages, math, and science. As a young man, he became one of Peter's most trusted aides. He spent five years in France, studying military engineering and also serving in the French army. There he was befriended by Voltaire, who referred to him as the "dark star of Russia's enlightenment," and by Diderot, whom, fifty years later, he would introduce to Catherine the Great. On his return to Russia, Gannibal was appointed "principal translator of foreign books at the Imperial Court." But he did more than translate books about scientific and military matters; he also built fortifications all over Russia. One of these forts—Kronstadt in the Gulf of Finland—was still important over two hundred years later, during the Blockade of Leningrad.

After Peter's death, Gannibal lost his influence. Eventually he retired with his second wife to Mikhailovskoye, the estate granted him by the Empress Elizabeth. There, as Pushkin wrote in a note to *Eugene Onegin*, "the black African who had become a Russian noble lived out his life like a French *philosophe*." And it was there, during the summer of 1827, that Pushkin worked on *Peter the Great's African*. He had at least one meeting with Gannibal's last surviving son, who gave him some biographical notes about Gannibal, and he almost certainly heard stories about Gannibal from other surviving relatives and acquaintances.

Andrey Sinyavsky has written that Pushkin "seized upon his negroid appearance and his African past, which he loved perhaps more dearly than he did his aristocratic [Russian] ancestry."[4] This points to an interesting paradox. Feeling himself to be an outsider, Pushkin defiantly identified with an ancestor he saw as still more of an outsider. Gannibal, however, was no ordinary outsider; he was a close aide to Peter the Great. Identifying with Gannibal allowed Pushkin, too, to be both outsider and insider. And this, no doubt, helped him to write more freely about one of Russia's strangest and most intimidating rulers.

Pushkin also, on occasion, uses Gannibal as a mouthpiece for more personal confessions. As a young man, Pushkin was a superstar of his day. In passages such as the following, he is clearly writing about himself:

People usually looked upon the young black man as some kind of wonder, clustering around him and showering him with greetings and questions. This general curiosity—veiled though it was by an air of goodwill—wounded his self-esteem. [...] He felt that women saw him as some kind of rare beast, a peculiar, alien creature accidentally transported to a world with which it had nothing in common. Indeed, he envied people who went entirely unnoticed, thinking them fortunate in their dullness.[5]

And there are many other parallels. The kind, charming, and socially irreproachable Countess D.—Gannibal's Parisian love—has much in common with Yelizaveta Vorontsova, probably the most important of Pushkin's many loves. And just as Gannibal returns to Petersburg, accepting the inevitable loss of the Countess D. and of his sophisticated, erotically charged life in Paris, so Pushkin himself returns to northern Russia, parting with both Vorontsova and the southern charm of Odessa. And as Gannibal embraces the "noble ambition" of working alongside Peter the Great to help fashion a new Russia, so Pushkin, at least for a few years in the late 1820s, hoped to work alongside Nicholas I and, through his poetry, help to shape Russia's destiny.

The novel begins with a contrast between Russia and France: the first chapter is set in Paris, where Ibrahim (as Pushkin calls him) lives the luxurious life of the corrupt and unproductive French elite. Voltaire and Montesquieu receive a brief mention, but Pushkin puts more emphasis on the sexual and financial scandals of the time. In the second chapter, Ibrahim returns to Petersburg, to "the newborn capital being conjured from the swamp by autocracy." He imagines the entire country as one "vast factory where only machines were in motion, where every worker was carrying out his work according to a well-established routine." Everywhere Ibrahim looks, "wooden bridges and canals without embankments testified to the recent triumph of human will over the resistance of nature."

The other important contrast is between the modernizers and the boyars—that is, the old Russian nobility. Pushkin reproduces the Frenchified language of members of the Petersburg elite and the folksy, idiomatic language of the boyars. He shows us the traditional clothes worn by the boyars' families in their own homes and the newfangled attire they have to wear during their compulsory attendance at Peter's new "Assemblies." We see "artful attempts" on the part of elderly ladies "to combine the new manner of dress with the now-outlawed styles of the past." Still more vividly, the measured pace of boyar life is set against the way that Korsakov, a foppish courtier just back from Paris, is constantly dashing about, endangering himself by his lack of forethought. Korsakov, unsurprisingly, evokes the boyars' contempt; they refer to him as "a French monkey." Ibrahim, on the other hand, wins their respect—because of his dignified poise and because he treats *them* with respect.

At one point, Peter says, "Listen, Ibrahim, you're all alone here, without kith or kin. You're a stranger to everyone but myself. If I should die today, what would become of you, my poor African? You need to establish yourself while there's still time, to find support in new connections. You need to ally with the Russian boyars." Peter then offers to matchmake on Ibrahim's behalf. The real Peter did not matchmake on Gannibal's behalf, but he did matchmake for one of his orderlies—an example of how, throughout the novel, Pushkin's concern is with historical plausibility, not with literal historical accuracy.

The planned marriage symbolizes what both Pushkin and Peter understand to be Ibrahim's main role: he is to mediate between the old and the new, between Russia and France. Svetlana Evdokimova writes,

> The idea of mediation between Russia and the West was very dear to Pushkin. Moreover, mediation in general is a central concern of Pushkin's philosophy and his works … In his own life too, Pushkin wanted to mediate between his friends, the Decembrists, and the regime. Pushkin's ideal characters, therefore, are always able to mediate between the two opposite realms of reality and to establish a new order.[6]

An unfinished work by a great writer inevitably provokes much discussion. Often, critics assume that the author was dissatisfied with what he had written. In *Peter the Great's African*, however, Pushkin manages to say a great deal in a short space and he published most of the two central chapters during his lifetime. Together, these two extracts—the accounts of Peter's assembly and of the feast-day dinner at the Rzhevskys—present us with a vivid picture of the social changes that were Pushkin's main concern in this work. Pushkin may have abandoned the novel simply because he felt that he had already said all he could say in this genre. To say more, he would need to turn either to narrative poetry—to *Poltava* and *The Bronze Horseman*—or to more detailed archival study.

There are, of course, many other plausible hypotheses. One of the most interesting is that any continuation of the novel would have required a fuller treatment of Ibrahim's blackness. We know from a diary entry by Pushkin's friend, Alexey Vulf, that Pushkin's original plan was for Ibrahim to marry Natalya and then, when she gives birth to a white child, send her off to a monastery.[7] This *Othello* theme certainly preoccupied Pushkin deeply; it surfaces unexpectedly in several of his works, not only in *Poltava*, written shortly after *Peter the Great's African*, but also in *The Egyptian Nights*, written in 1835. Pushkin was proud of his black ancestor and he saw his own "black blood" as a source of his creativity. Yet he seems also to have been afraid that his own "blackness" might, in the end, overwhelm him. Pushkin always thought of himself as ugly; even before his marriage to a famously beautiful and much younger wife, he seems to have been afraid of acting out the part of a Russian Othello. And throughout his life nearly everyone around him—friends and enemies alike—spoke in a simplistic way of his "African blood." His close friend Pyotr Vyazemsky, for example, wrote as Pushkin lay dying, "His fiery and passionate soul and his African blood could not withstand the irritation produced by the doubts and suspicions of society."[8] It is possible that Pushkin felt unable to continue the novel because he found his original plan too disturbing, too close to home.[9] And if so, it hardly needs saying that these fears, in the end, proved only too justified.

2

In 1830, when Pushkin became engaged to Natalya Goncharova, his father gave him the village of Kisteniovo, part of the family's Boldino estate near Nizhny Novgorod. Now a landowner for the first time, Pushkin traveled to Boldino early that autumn, in order to have two hundred serfs officially transferred to his name. Quarantine regulations imposed in response to a cholera outbreak prevented him from returning to Moscow and he was obliged—to his intense frustration—to stay in the village until early December.

During these months—now known as the "Boldino Autumn"—Pushkin wrote an astonishing number of masterpieces. Among them was *The Tales of Belkin*—five seemingly simple anecdotes supposedly narrated by Ivan Petrovich Belkin, an unsophisticated village squire. On completing this—his first finished work of fictional prose—Pushkin at once embarked on another work in the voice of this same Belkin, *The History of the Village of Goriukhino*.

Belkin begins the main part of his "History" by stating that the foundation and first settlement of Goriukhino is enveloped by "the dark of obscurity"—an obvious tautology that he has already used in another context. The American scholars David M. Bethea and Sergei Davydov have pointed out that the same "dark of obscurity" seems to have enveloped *The History of the Village of Goriukhino* itself.[10] No one knows for sure how Pushkin intended to continue it and why he left it unfinished. There is, in fact, no absolute agreement about when he wrote it; at least one scholar has argued that it was written not in 1830 but in 1835. Even the spelling of the village's name is unstable. Pushkin spells it thirty times as "Goriukhino," but five times as "Gorokhino." Most editions—whether in Russian or in other languages—render the spelling consistent, but, even in his unfinished works, Pushkin is seldom careless about detail. The inconsistency is almost certainly intended—though not, of course, by the often thoughtless Belkin.

"Goriukhino" is derived from the word *gore*, meaning "grief." "Gorokhino," on the other hand, points us towards Tsar Gorokh—a legendary figure who presided over some long-ago golden age. *The History of Goriukhino*, then, was conceived as the history of a fortunate village that had existed from immemorial times. Gradually, however, it had grown impoverished—and so become known not as Gorokhino but as Goriukhino.[11]

There is a consensus that *Goriukhino* contains a great deal of parody, but there is less agreement about the purpose and target of this parody. There is no doubt that Pushkin parodies several Russian historians he looked down upon. A little surprisingly, Pushkin also, at least once, parodies Nikolay Karamzin, whose twelve-volume *History of the Russian State* he admired. What is probably more important is that there are many respects in which Belkin is a parody of Pushkin himself.

Like Belkin, Pushkin belongs to a now impoverished noble family. Like Belkin, he felt bored and lonely in the depths of the country and could find little to do but write; not intending to stay in Boldino for long, he had taken only three books with him—Nikolay Gnedich's translation of the *Iliad*, an anthology of English poetry, and Polevoy's *History of the Russian People*. Like Belkin, he tried his hand at almost every literary genre. And like Belkin, he had come to set more and more value on the writing of history.

Belkin writes, "The possibility of moving from trivial and questionable tales to the narration of true and great events had long stirred my imagination. A writer could achieve nothing higher, I believed, than to be the judge, observer, and prophet of peoples and epochs." Here, as elsewhere, Pushkin is questioning the limits of a historian's remit. Like Belkin, he wanted to narrate "true and great events," though he would never, writing in his own voice, have used such high-flown language. On the other hand, he did not—despite his famous poem "The Prophet" (1826)—aspire to be a sociopolitical prophet, nor did he imagine himself as a judge. It is not—he believed— a historian's "business to justify or accuse […]. His business is to resurrect a past age in all its truth."[12]

Pushkin had read not only Karamzin but also Augustin Thierry and the other French Romantic, liberal historians of Thierry's generation. In some respects, Pushkin admired their work, but he was critical of their grandiosity and their tendency to deny the role played during historical crises by blind chance. These historians were so eager—he believed—to grasp the *meaning* of a past age that they often exaggerated the role of the fundamental historical laws they claimed to have discovered.

Pushkin was still more critical of Russian followers of these French historians. Russia—in Pushkin's view—had its distinct pattern of historical development. Understandings derived from the study of western European countries were often irrelevant. And Russia's general instability had allowed chance events to play an even more important role than in the history of more stable countries. Through the figure of Belkin—one of the most amateurish of all fictional historians—Pushkin mocks the scientific aspirations of such historians as Nikolay Polevoy. Belkin thinks he is being scientific, yet almost every step of his research is determined by chance. First comes the "chance discovery" of a basket of old yearbooks. Then a kite—in Russian, *vozdushny zmei* (a snake of the air!)—"fashioned from a chronicle"—lands in his yard. It is also only too clear that Belkin has a poor understanding of the boundary between history and fiction. In what purports to be a work of historical scholarship his frequent use of dashes to disguise names and dates is absurd.

A very different kind of historian—a model that Pushkin may have hoped to emulate—was Pimen, the humble monk and chronicler in his historical drama *Boris Godunov* (1825/1831). Sergei Davydov refers to Pimen as looking at the past "with that supreme poise [...] which Pushkin himself strove to achieve." And in a letter to his friend Anton Delvig, Pushkin wrote, "In [Pimen] I collected features that had captivated me in our old chronicles: naiveté, touching humility, something both child-like and wise, an almost devout zeal for the power of the tsar given to him by God. [...] It seemed to me that this character was at once new and familiar to the Russian heart."[13]

Just as Belkin shares some of Pushkin's life story, so the village of Goriukhino is modeled on Boldino. For many years, the Boldino estate had yielded little but had, at least, been left alone by its owners. In 1825, Pushkin's father had appointed a new steward, Mikhailo Kalashnikov, who in 1826 managed to extract over thirteen thousand rubles from the peasants. Kalashnikov also stole a great deal for himself, and the village, like the fictional Goriukhino, became destitute within three years; in 1829, it yielded only 1,639 rubles. The Boldino peasants, like those of Goriukhino, lodged an official complaint, but it was difficult for Pushkin to respond to this. He was not in a position to treat Kalashnikov with any severity; not only had he fathered a child by Kalashnikov's daughter but he also desperately needed money in order to marry. In the words of Paul Debreczeny, from whom much of the above is summarized, "he was now a feudal lord whose interest it was to squeeze as much out of his peasants as he could."[14]

The Boldino autumn marked a crisis in almost every aspect of Pushkin's life. He was struggling to find a way of earning money from his writing. He was saying an inner goodbye to past loves, preparing to give up his bachelor life for a marriage about which he had deep apprehensions. The recent death of his uncle, the minor poet Vasily L'vovich Pushkin, had been a reminder to him of his own mortality. And, more directly than ever before, he was being confronted with the realities of serfdom and his own dependence upon its injustices.

Goriukhino is perhaps best understood as a series of questions Pushkin was asking himself at this turning point in his life. The parody of other historians may have been a way for him to try on different styles and viewpoints as he moved towards his own, more original way of writing history. And the self-parody constitutes an often critical self-examination on Pushkin's part—above all, with regard to his treatment of his own serfs. *Goriukhino* breaks off on a note of deep, tragic seriousness. It may well have been Pushkin's awareness of the bleakness of his peasants' position that made it impossible for him to continue in a way that would have been acceptable to the censorship of his day. It is also possible that Pushkin realized that his understandings needed to be embodied in some other form. *Goriukhino* can be considered an experiment. Its true completion—several years later—came in *The Captain's Daughter* and *The History of Pugachov*.

3

Pushkin worked on *Dubrovsky* between October 1832 and February 1833. Like *The Captain's Daughter* (1836), it is an account of a seemingly inevitable conflict and a plea for the importance of reconciliation.

The Dubrovskys, like the Belkins, are modeled on Pushkin's own family. The Dubrovsky estate, Kisteniovka, bears almost the same name as a village belonging to Pushkin's father: Kisteniovo. Both the Pushkins and the Dubrovskys belong to the now marginalized old aristocracy. Both families have had to pay for their honorable conduct during various crises in Russian political history. In 1762 the woman we know as Catherine the Great (then the empress consort) deposed her husband Peter III and had herself proclaimed empress. Lev Pushkin (the poet's grandfather) remained loyal to Peter III and suffered for this. The elder Dubrovsky evidently did the same.

The long, overcomplicated, atrociously written legal document that allows Troyekurov to dispossess Dubrovsky is a transcript of a real judgment made by a Russian court in 1832; Pushkin introduces this document with fierce irony, changing only names and dates. Given the corruption of the legal system, there is little hope for a solution to the worsening conflict. Dubrovsky's old nurse believes that the tsar will put everything right, but the tsar, needless to say, is unlikely to have heard of the small village of Kisteniovka. The only benign patriarch, paradoxically, is the young Dubrovsky—he behaves generously both towards some of his potential victims and towards the former family serfs who constitute his band of brigands.

Words such as "war," "enemy," and "brigand" are bandied about from the very beginning of the quarrel between Dubrovsky and Troyekurov; even the name of the Dubrovskys' estate, Kisteniovka, is derived from the word *kisten'*, meaning "flail" or "bludgeon." Troyekurov and the elder Dubrovsky are dangerously similar; both find it hard to compromise or forgive. Vladimir Dubrovsky is little different; what turns him into a rebel is his pride and fearlessness. These same qualities, however, endear him, in his disguise as French tutor, to the young Masha—and it is his love of Masha that enables him to forgive Troyekurov and so break the vicious circle of pride and vengefulness. The conflict between the Troyekurovs and the Dubrovskys is not as fated as it may seem.

We have only the briefest of indications as to how Pushkin meant *Dubrovsky* to continue. One note runs: "Life of Maria Kirilovna.

Death of Prince Vereisky. The widow. The Englishman. Meeting. Gamblers. The chief of police. Conclusion." The other runs: "Moscow, a healer, solitude. Tavern, denunciation. Suspicions, the chief of police." "The Englishman" may well be yet another manifestation of Dubrovsky, but the nature of Pushkin's intended conclusion remains a mystery.

Dubrovsky addresses several themes that were important to Pushkin and that he went on to treat more fully in *The Captain's Daughter*: peasant revolt, the decline of the old nobility, and the importance of forgiveness. It is possible that Pushkin abandoned *Dubrovsky* because of an ambiguity in its central plot; it is unclear whether the Dubrovsky serfs choose to side with the young Dubrovsky out of feudal loyalty to their master or because they are ripe for revolt. Pushkin may also have felt unable to fuse the different parts of the novel into a satisfactory whole; he seems to have been more interested in the study of Russian social conditions that takes up many of the earlier chapters than in the somewhat stereotyped romance that follows. Even at the level of style, the earlier chapters are more interesting; the language is both more richly idiomatic and more syntactically complex.

Nevertheless, *Dubrovsky* remains a gripping story. The swiftly changing narrative viewpoint and Pushkin's mastery of telling detail make it one of the most vivid pictures we have of provincial Russia in the late eighteenth or early nineteenth centuries. And in the words of Prince Mirsky, from his classic *History of Russian Literature,* "Had it been finished, it would have been the best Russian novel of action."[15]

4

The Egyptian Nights is a masterpiece. First published not long after Pushkin's death, it consists of three chapters of prose, written in autumn 1835, and two passages of verse. The first passage of verse incorporates lines from the unfinished narrative poem "Yezersky" (1832–33); the second is an expansion of a poem about Cleopatra that

Pushkin drafted in 1824 and revised in 1828. Pushkin would almost certainly have developed the verse passages further had he gone on to complete *The Egyptian Nights*. The three prose sections also represent a reworking of a theme—the "Cleopatra of the Neva"—that had long preoccupied Pushkin. This theme appears first in a fragment written in 1828, and then, for a second time, in "We were spending the evening at the dacha" (1835).

In the first chapter of *The Egyptian Nights* Pushkin tells us that Charsky's life "could have been most pleasant; but he had the misfortune to write and publish poetry." The ensuing account of Charsky's awkward relationship to his vocation is fascinating—all the more so since Charsky clearly represents some aspects of Pushkin himself. Like Pushkin, he is proud, independent-minded and greatly irritated by society's misunderstanding of poetry. And like Pushkin, Charsky at least sometimes knows the "state of grace when fancies outline themselves clearly before you and you discover vivid, unexpected words to embody your visions, when verses flow readily from your pen and resonant rhymes come forward to meet orderly thoughts."

In the second chapter, the improvvisatore offers to perform for Charsky. Charsky provocatively suggests that he improvise on the theme "It is for the poet to choose the matter of his songs himself; the crowd has no right to direct his inspiration." The Italian rises to the challenge. His success is, of course, paradoxical. His poem asserts the poet's absolute freedom to write as he pleases; by obeying a demand imposed from outside, he does the opposite of what his words so eloquently assert.

In the third chapter, after a succession of awkward moments, a majestic, Cleopatra-like beauty reads aloud the theme: *"Cleopatra e i suoi amanti,"* Cleopatra and her lovers. A repeated motif of the story is the interdependency of poise and awkwardness. Both Charsky and the improvvisatore slip between extremes of deep awkwardness and poised fluency. And the majestic beauty is contrasted with a plain, bashful girl whom everyone, for no apparent reason, assumes to have first proposed the theme of Cleopatra.

There are both real and literary prototypes for the improvvisatore.

Pushkin owned a copy of Samuel Taylor Coleridge's short dramatic piece *The Improvisatore* (1827), and he would certainly have known Vladimir Odoevsky's story "The Improvisatore" (1833). More importantly, he knew the great Polish poet Adam Mickiewicz, who was a brilliant improviser and whose performances caused a sensation in both Moscow and Petersburg. According to an account of a party in Moscow in autumn 1826, Pushkin exclaimed, on hearing one of Mickiewicz's improvisations, "'What genius! What sacred fire! What am I compared to him?' and, throwing himself on Adam's neck, embraced him and began to kiss him like a brother."[16] Later, in the early 1830s, the issue of Polish independence came between the two poets, but even their bitter disagreements proved fruitful to Pushkin. Mickiewicz's criticisms of Russian imperialism in his long poem "Digression" (1832) provided a crucial inspiration for one of Pushkin's greatest works, *The Bronze Horseman*.

The rights and wrongs of Russian imperialism lie outside the scope of *The Egyptian Nights*. What matters is that Charsky needs the improvvisatore, just as Pushkin needed Mickiewicz. Mickiewicz prompted Pushkin towards a deeper understanding of what Petersburg stands for in Russian culture and history—and it is possible that the improvvisatore may help Charsky—and Pushkin himself—to a more fruitful understanding of the poet's place in society. Charsky is ill at ease with the Italian's theatricality and greed, but his own attempt to separate his art from the outside world is failing; he is unable to resolve what has been described as "the conflict between social position, literary commerce, and inspiration."[17]

Pushkin had left government service in the mid-1820s and was trying to make a living from writing. The question of what can legitimately be bought and sold was of urgent concern to him. The old system of patronage was no longer viable, but Pushkin felt uncomfortable about depending on the marketplace. In the short poem "Conversation between a Bookseller and a Poet," he had attempted to resolve his uncertainties through the formula, "Inspiration is not for sale, but one can sell a manuscript." In *The Egyptian Nights*, however, he presents us with a more complex picture. Cleopatra sells

her body and the improvvisatore sells his inspiration, yet both somehow remain independent. Charsky, on the other hand, tries doggedly
to safeguard his privacy and independence but meets with little success. Pushkin provides no answers in *The Egyptian Nights*, but he
poses many important questions.

The Egyptian Nights is dense with delicate parallels and paradoxes.
Like the improvvisatore, Cleopatra's lovers are called upon to surrender themselves. And Cleopatra herself—also like the improvvisatore—is an inspired artist, able to divine a man's hidden wishes. There
is even a suggestion, in the very last line—as she looks "with eyes
surprised by tenderness" at the youngest of the three men who take
up her challenge—that love may compel her, too, to surrender herself.
How Pushkin intended to develop the parallel between the historical
Cleopatra and the majestic Petersburg beauty is unclear. As for the
prickly Charsky, he has already had to yield in several small ways. It
seems likely that he will be compelled to let go of still more of his
defenses.

Two attempts have been made to complete *The Egyptian Nights*,
but both destroy the delicate equilibrium of the original. The Symbol-
ist poet Valery Bryusov concluded the work by continuing the Cleopatra poem; an account of her three nights with her doomed lovers is
followed by the arrival of Mark Anthony. Here the emphasis is on
Cleopatra's stark, courageous sexuality. The émigré poet and Pushkin
scholar Modest Gofman, on the other hand, saw the verse as second-
ary and attempted to construct a complete prose text, using both
passages from the earlier "Cleopatra of the Neva" fragments and some
additions of his own. There is also *That Third Guy*, a farce written in
1937 by Sigizmund Krzhizhanovsky (1887–1950) and set in a Rome
that has become a police state; the "third guy" (a bad poet) is the third
and youngest of Cleopatra's three lovers, on the run from the security
police. *That Third Guy*, however, is a freestanding work—a fantasy
on a theme from Pushkin rather than a serious attempt to reconstruct
The Egyptian Nights.

All this can be seen as testimony to the resonance of *The Egyptian*

Nights. The questions it raises stay in the minds of readers. And, if it ends abruptly, we could say that, like Shakespeare's Cleopatra, Pushkin "makes hungry / Where most [he] satisfies."

—ROBERT CHANDLER

NOTES ON RUSSIAN NAMES

A RUSSIAN has three names: a first name, a patronymic, and a family name. A person's patronymic is derived from the first name of their father. Thus, the son of Andrey Gavrilovich Dubrovsky is called Vladimir Andreyevich Dubrovsky, and the daughter of Kirila Petrovich Troyekurov is called Maria Kirilovna Troyekurova. The full form of a Russian first name is almost never used on its own. In order to show respect, one calls a person by their first name and patronymic; Troyekurov, for example, is usually addressed as "Kirila Petrovich."

Close friends or relatives usually address each other by one of the many diminutive, or affectionate, forms of their first names. Masha, for example, is a diminutive of Maria, just as Grisha is a diminutive of Grigory. Less obviously, Vanya is a diminutive of Ivan, and Volodya and Volodka are both diminutives of Vladimir. A diminutive is not necessarily shorter than the equivalent Christian name—Arkhipushka, for example, is a diminutive of Arkhip.

Married or older peasants are often addressed and referred to by the patronymic alone, or by a slightly abbreviated form of it. Thus Orina Yegorovna Byzyreva, the former nurse of the elder Dubrovsky, is usually referred to simply as Yegorovna. The postmaster and his wife in *Dubrovsky* address each other as Pakhomovna and Sidorych. Similarly, the priest's wife in *Dubrovsky* is referred to as Fedotovna, and the fool in *Peter the Great's African* as Yekimovna.

FURTHER READING

Hugh Barnes, *Gannibal: The Moor of Petersburg* (Profile Books, 2005).

David M. Bethea, *The Pushkin Handbook* (University of Wisconsin Press, 2013).

David M. Bethea and Sergei Davydov, "The [Hi]story of the Village Gorjuxino: In Praise of Pushkin's Folly," in *The Slavic and East European Journal*, vol. 28, no. 3 (Autumn 1984), pp. 291–309.

T. J. Binyon, *Pushkin: A Biography* (HarperCollins, 2002).

Robert Chandler, *A Short Life of Pushkin* (Pushkin Press, 2017).

Robert Chandler, ed., *Russian Magic Tales from Pushkin to Platonov* (Penguin Classics, 2012).

Robert Chandler, ed., *Russian Short Stories from Pushkin to Buida* (Penguin Classics, 2005).

Robert Chandler, Boris Dralyuk, and Irina Mashinski, eds., *The Penguin Book of Russian Poetry* (Penguin Classics, 2015).

Paul Debreczeny, *The Other Pushkin: A Study of Alexander Pushkin's Prose Fiction* (Stanford University Press, 1983).

Svetlana Evdokimova, *Pushkin's Historical Imagination* (Yale University Press, 1999).

N. K. Gei, *Pushkin—prozaik (Pushkin as a Prose Writer)* (IMLI RAN, 2008).

Maksim Hanukai, "The Disenchantment of Poetry: Pushkin's *Egyptian Nights*," *Ulbandus Review*, vol. 12 (2009–2010), pp. 63–82.

Lindsey Hughes, *Russia in the Age of Peter the Great* (Yale University Press, 1998).

Andrew Kahn, ed., *The Cambridge Companion to Pushkin* (Cambridge University Press, 2006).

Sigizmund Krzhizhanovsky, *That Third Guy: A Comedy from the Stalinist 1930s with Essays on Theater* (University of Wisconsin Press, 2018).

D. S. Mirsky, *A History of Russian Literature*, ed. Francis J. Whitfield (Routledge & Kegan Paul, 1968).

D. S. Mirsky, *Pushkin* (Dutton, 1963).

Catharine Theimer Nepomnyashchy, Nicole Svobodny, and Ludmilla A. Trigos, eds., *Under the Sky of My Africa: Alexander Pushkin and Blackness* (Northwestern University Press, 2006).

Alexander Pushkin, *Belkin's Stories and A History of Goryúkhino Village*, trans. Roger Clarke (Alma Classics, 2014).

Alexander Pushkin, *The Captain's Daughter*, trans. Robert Chandler and Elizabeth Chandler (NYRB Classics, 2014).

Alexander Pushkin, *Eugene Onegin*, trans. Stanley Mitchell (Penguin Classics, 2008).

Alexander Pushkin, *The Gypsies and Other Narrative Poems*, trans. Antony Wood (Angel Classics, 2013).

Alexander Pushkin, *Povesti Belkina* (IMLI RAN/Nasledie, 1999)—a scholarly edition of the Russian text, with commentary.

Alexander Pushkin, *The Queen of Spades and Other Stories*, ed. Andrew Kahn, trans. Alan Myers (Oxford World's Classics, 1997)—includes a good translation of the *Tales of the Late Ivan Petrovich Belkin*.

J. Thomas Shaw, ed., *The Letters of Alexander Pushkin* (Indiana University Press, 1963).

Andrei Sinyavsky, *Strolls with Pushkin*, trans. Catharine Theimer Nepomnyashchy and Slava I. Yastremski (Columbia University Press, 2017).

William Mills Todd III, *Fiction and Society in the Age of Pushkin* (Harvard University Press, 1986).

ACKNOWLEDGMENTS

My thanks to the following, all of whom have made useful suggestions: Maria Bloshteyn, Leon Burnett, Lucy Chandler, Olive Classe, Simon Dixon, Masha Dmitrovskaya, Irina Mashinski, Olga Meerson, Mark Miller. Many of my thoughts about Dubrovsky are taken from a fine article by N. Zhilina, published in the *Baltiiskii filologicheskii kurier*, vol. 1 (Kaliningrad, 2000).

—R.C.

NOTES

PREFACE

1 Andrey Sinyavsky, *Progulki s Pushkinym* (Petersburg: Vsemirnoe slovo, 1993), pp. 69–70.

2 Quoted in Paul Debreczeny, *The Other Pushkin: A Study of Alexander Pushkin's Prose Fiction* (Stanford University Press, 1983), p. 34.

PETER THE GREAT'S AFRICAN

1 From "Ala," by Nikolay Yazykov (1803–1846). Yazykov was a friend of Pushkin's.

2 From "N. N.'s Journey to Paris and London," by Ivan Dmitriev (1760–1837). Andrew Kahn writes, "The anonymous traveller lampooned in the poem for his excessive enthusiasm about visiting Paris and London is Pushkin's uncle, Vasily L'vovich Pushkin (1770–1830), a minor poet and member of [Nikolay] Karamzin's circle." Alexander Pushkin, *The Queen of Spades and Other Stories*, ed. Andrew Kahn, trans. Alan Myers (Oxford World's Classics, 1997), p. 266.

3 The War of the Spanish Succession (1701–14).

4 The Duke of Orléans, nephew of Louis XIV, ruled as regent until Louis XV reached adulthood.

5 John Law (1671–1729) was a Scottish economist and expert gambler who served as Controller General of Finances of France under the Duke of Orléans. He was a strong advocate of paper currency. Some of the investors in his Mississippi Company, which held a monopoly on business in the French colonies, grew so fabulously wealthy—on paper—that a new term was coined to describe them: "millionaires." The wild speculation inspired by the company, and by Law's policies, eventually led to economic collapse, panic, and riots; when the "Mississippi Bubble" burst in 1720, Law had to flee Paris.

6   Armand, Duke of Richelieu (1696–1788), the grandnephew of the fa-
     mous Cardinal, portrayed the life of the court in his memoirs.

7   From Voltaire's *La Pucelle d'Orléans*, Chant XIII (1730–1762), in
     Charles William Bury's translation of 1796–97. Pushkin, rather than
     translating, quotes the original:

> *Temps fortuné, marqué par la licence,*
> *Où la folie, agitant son grelot,*
> *D'un pied léger parcourt toute la France,*
> *Où nul mortel ne daigne être dévot,*
> *Où l'on fait tout excepté pénitence.*

8   Voltaire, born François-Marie Arouet (1694–1778); Guillaume Amfrye
     de Chaulieu (1639–1720) was a poet renowned for his wit; Montesquieu
     (1689–1755) was an Enlightenment political philosopher; and Bernard
     Le Bovier de Fontenelle (1657–1757), the permanent secretary of the
     Académie Française, was widely admired for his writings on scientific
     topics.

9   From "On the Death of Prince Meshchersky" (1779), by Gavrila Der-
     zhavin (1743–1816), translated by Peter France, in Robert Chandler, Bo-
     ris Dralyuk, and Irina Mashinski, eds., *The Penguin Book of Russian
     Poetry* (Penguin Classics, 2015), p. 11. Derzhavin was the greatest Rus-
     sian poet before Pushkin.

10   Military units stationed in Petersburg were usually transferred in sum-
     mer to this small nearby town.

11   Before Peter the Great banned it during his Westernizing reforms, the
     kaftan was a standard item of Russian male dress. The ban was rescinded
     during the nineteenth century, but kaftans continued to be seen as pro-
     vincial or old-fashioned.

12   Peter the Great's second wife, a Polish Lithuanian peasant who took the
     name Catherine on converting to Russian Orthodoxy. In 1724, Peter
     had her crowned empress.

13   This is Peter the Great's daughter. From 1741 till 1762 she will reign as
     empress.

14   Peter the Great's decisive victory over Charles XII of Sweden at the
     Battle of Poltava (1709) was the most important battle in the Great
     Northern War (1700–1721). It confirmed Russia's status as a major Eu-
     ropean power.

15   Prince Alexander Danilovich Menshikov (1673–1729) rose from hum-
     ble origins to become one of Peter's closest aides. He amassed a fortune

and came to hold many important titles; he was noted for his corruption, which on occasion angered Peter. Yakov Dolgoruky (1639–1720), a member of the old Russian nobility, was a statesman and general. He survived ten years' captivity in Sweden and was known for his loyalty and honesty. Robert Bruce (1668–1720), known as Roman Vilimovich Bruce, of Scottish descent, commanded the Russian artillery during the Battle of Poltava and served as the first chief commander of St. Petersburg. Yefim Raguzinsky (1691–1749) was the nephew of the Serbian merchant who, as Russian ambassador to the Ottoman Empire, had purchased the young Ibrahim and had him sent to Russia; he rose to the rank of lieutenant general.

16   Anthony De Vière was, by one account, a Portuguese Jew who made his way to St. Petersburg on a merchant ship. Peter appointed him the city's general chief of police in 1718.

17   From the tragedy *Argivyane* (1822–25), by Wilhelm Küchelbecker (1797–1846), a schoolmate and friend of Pushkin's.

18   Boris Sheremetev (1652–1719) was a field marshal during the Great Northern War against Sweden. Count Feodor Golovin (1650–1706), also a field marshal, became the first Chancellor of the Russian Empire. Unlike Sheremetev, Golovin was very close to Peter.

19   Ivan Ivanovich Buturlin (1661–1738) was a distinguished general.

20   Feofan Prokopovich (1681–1736), a theologian and man of letters, impressed Peter with his eloquence and helped implement his controversial religious reforms. Ilya Kopievich (or Kopievsky) (1651–1714) was a Belarusian printer, based in Amsterdam, who supplied Peter with foreign books. Gavril Buzhinsky (1680–1731), another senior churchman, was also a supporter of Peter's religious reforms.

21   Boris Korsakov (1702–57) studied naval matters in France from 1716 until 1724.

22   In 1718, by special decree, Peter the Great founded his so-called "Assemblies"—the prototype of aristocratic balls. Peter held Assemblies himself, and other members of the aristocracy were expected to do the same. They were an important part of Peter's modernization program—until then, Russian women had seldom taken part in any aspect of public life. Like all Peter's reforms, however, their introduction was carried out with extreme coercion. On some occasions, at least, Peter had guards posted at the doors, to prevent guests from leaving early. See Lindsey Hughes, *Russia in the Age of Peter the Great* (Yale University Press, 1998), p. 187.

23 The boyars were the hereditary Russian nobility. As part of his modernization project, Peter introduced a new system of ranks and titles. All members of the nobility were required to perform some kind of government service, and commoners who reached a certain rank in the army, navy, or civil service were automatically ennobled. These reforms, needless to say, were not welcomed by all.

24 In 1698, Peter established the Order of St. Andrew, the country's highest order of chivalry. It was worn as a light-blue sash.

25 At first, only wind orchestras played at Assemblies. String orchestras were introduced later.

26 Natalya Kirilovna Naryshkina (1651–96) was the mother of Peter the Great.

27 Most of this chapter, from "In a large room lit by tallow candles" (p. 20) to this point, was first published separately, under the title "An Assembly in the Days of Peter I," in *Literaturnaya gazeta* (Literary Gazette), 1830, no. 13.

28 From Pushkin's first long poem, a fairy tale (1820).

29 During the Great Northern War, Russia and Sweden fought two battles at Narva. Russia lost the first, in 1700, but won the second, in 1704. Many of the Swedish officers taken prisoner in the course of the war remained in Russia a long time; some earned their living as fencing teachers, language teachers, or dancing masters.

30 As a student at the Imperial Lycée, Pushkin had two nicknames: "the Frenchman" and "the monkey." Korsakov is often seen as a mere figure of fun, but it seems likely that he is a part of Pushkin, that he represents Pushkin's aspiration, as a young man, to become perfectly modern, sophisticated, and Western (with thanks to Maria Bloshteyn for drawing our attention to these nicknames).

31 The order of precedence (*mestnichestvo*) had been abolished in 1682. Its most obvious manifestation had been in the order of seating at the tsar's table. More importantly, it had dictated which government posts a boyar could occupy. This complicated system was based both on the individual's seniority within a particular extended aristocratic family and on the order of precedence of the various families, the latter being calculated according to lineage records dating back to 1475. *Mestnichestvo* was an obstacle to reformers, since it could prevent gifted people from being appointed to an important state post. As the autocracy developed, the role of this system was progressively reduced.

32 That is, a headdress that entirely concealed the hair—an example of the items of clothing that Peter's Europeanizing reforms attempted to eliminate.

33 I.e., "a dress with a dome-shaped skirt. The Russian is *robrond*, from the French *robe ronde*.

34 Peter the Great saw beards as a symbol of the old ways he wanted to eliminate. All men attending his court were required by an edict of 1689 to shave off their beards.

35 Lindsey Hughes quotes from a 1717 etiquette manual: "Of all the virtues which adorn well-born ladies or maidens and are required of them, meekness is the leading and chief virtue." *Russia in the Age of Peter the Great*, p. 193.

36 More precisely, "sourish shchi" (*kislye shchi*), a fizzy, fermented drink similar to mead. It was popular in Russian in the eighteenth and nineteenth centuries and was usually kept in champagne bottles. There were six ingredients: buckwheat, honey, either wheat or rye flour, and three kinds of malt—barley, rye, and wheat. "Shchi" is the old Russian word for "six."

37 Lindsey Hughes quotes from an article by a Slavophile commentator (1864): "Above all the apparent jollity and revelry of life there reigned the iron will of the head pedagogue (*pervovospitatel'*), which knew no bounds—everyone made merry by decree and even to the sound of drumbeats, they got drunk and made merry under compulsion." *Russia in the Age of Peter the Great*, p. 269.

38 See the Epistle of Paul to the Ephesians, 5:33.

39 Here, as elsewhere, the boyars use the word "German" of everyone and everything foreign that was not obviously French or Slav; it was, in fact, English merchants who had been granted the right to trade in tobacco. Until 1697, tobacco had been banned in Russia as ungodly; the Church called it "the Devil's incense." Peter's Assemblies—the rooms full of dense clouds of tobacco smoke—were offensive in many ways.

40 Gavrila Afanasevich professes to be afraid that someone may inform on him, or repeat his words to a third party who may then inform on him. Nevertheless, he goes on to speak his mind; there is, perhaps, a ritualistic quality about his first words.

41 Most of this chapter, from "It was a feast day" (p. 25) to this point, was first published separately, under the title "Chapter 4 of a Historical

Novel," in the 1829 issue of the almanac *Severnye tsvety* (Northern Flowers). Together with the extract from Chapter 3, it was republished in 1834, in the volume *Stories Published by Alexander Pushkin*.

42 From Alexander Ablesimov's (1742–83) libretto for Mikhail Sokolovsky's comic opera *The Miller Who Was a Wizard, a Cheat, and a Matchmaker* (1779).

43 It was rumored that Prince Menshikov, who was of humble origin, sold pies in the street as a child.

44 Both Shein and Troyekurov were early supporters of Peter the Great.

45 As he struggled from the mid-1820s to make a living from writing, Pushkin was deeply concerned by the question of what can legitimately be bought and sold. For further discussion of this question, see p. 173–174 of the afterword to the present volume. In August 1830, Pushkin's enemy Faddey Bulgarin (1789–1859) published a feuilleton, joking about Gannibal having been bought for a bottle of rum. This enraged Pushkin; some Soviet scholars have even suggested that this feuilleton was the reason for Pushkin's inability to return to work on *Peter the Great's African*. See Catharine Theimer Nepomnyashchy, "The Telltale Black Baby," in Catharine Theimer Nepomnyashchy, Nicole Svobodny and Ludmilla A. Trigos, eds., *Under the Sky of My Africa: Alexander Pushkin and Blackness* (Northwestern University Press, 2006), pp. 163–64.

46 Prince Bova and Yeruslan Lazarevich were the heroes of illustrated chapbooks published in the seventeenth century for the newly emerging middle classes. Both have their origins in foreign tales—Bova in French medieval romances about the knight Beuve de Hanstone (Bevis of Hampton in English), and Yeruslan Lazarevich in Ferdowsi's Persian epic *Shahnameh*, in which the hero Rostam is compared to a lion (*arslan* in Persian). The early Romanovs read chapbooks about Bova in childhood, while Pushkin worked incidents about Yeruslan Lazarevich into his first epic poem, *Ruslan and Ludmila* (1820), and into his late fairy tales in verse, *The Tale of Tsar Saltan* (1831) and *The Tale of the Golden Cockerel* (1834).

47 According to Lindsey Hughes, "a key issue is whether 'new men and women' exchanged one form of slavery (submission to custom) for another (submission to the state). In the conventional form of writing petitions in seventeenth-century Russia, even the highest magnates referred to themselves as the sovereign's 'slaves' (*kholopy*), wrote their names in their diminutive form, and prostrated themselves at the ruler's feet. Peter

outlawed these practices, but without changing the fundamental relationship of ruler and nobles" (*Russia in the Age of Peter the Great*, p. 295).

48 More precisely, one of the Streltsy (literally, "shooters"), special infantry units created by Ivan the Terrible in the 1540s. In 1698, the Moscow Streltsy rose up against Peter. Their rebellion failed, and thousands were executed or exiled.

49 Ibrahim's attitude to Natalya strikingly anticipates Pushkin's attitude towards the Natalya he himself married several years after giving up work on this novel.

50 *J'aurais planté là* the old liar: I would have sent the old liar packing. *(Avoir) une petite santé*: (to be in) poor health. *Mijaurée*: an affected young woman.

51 Throughout his life, nearly everyone around Pushkin spoke in similar terms of his "African blood." His close friend Piotr Viazemsky, for example, wrote in a letter as Pushkin lay dying, "His fiery and passionate soul and his African blood could not withstand the irritation produced by the doubts and suspicions of society" (Nepomnyashchy, "Introduction: Was Pushkin Black and Does It Matter?" *Under the Sky of My Africa*, p. 11).

52 The *seni*—the unheated room located between the outer door or porch and the habitable room or rooms of any Russian house, from a peasant hut to a city palace. This provided insulation from the cold and was also used as a storage area.

THE HISTORY OF THE VILLAGE OF GORIUKHINO

1 This manual by N. G. Kurganov (1726–96) went through several editions. It included sample letters, proverbs, anecdotes, basic grammatical rules, and general information of all kinds. Kurganov was a professor of mathematics and navigation at Moscow University. His name derives from the word *kurgan*, meaning an ancient burial mound.

2 Pyotr Plemyannikov (d. 1775) served under the Empress Elizabeth, the daughter of Peter the Great. His surname is derived from *plemya*, meaning "tribe." Bethea and Davydov point out that Kurganov and Plemyannikov—the two names that appear on the first page of *Goriukhino*—are both linked to the concept of historical origin. See David M. Bethea and Sergei Davydov, "The [Hi]story of the Village Gorjuxino: In Praise of Pushkin's Folly," in *The Slavic and East European Journal*, vol. 28, no. 3 (Autumn 1984), pp. 291–309 (299).

3   The German historian Berthold Niebuhr (1776–1831) is considered one
     of the founders of modern historical scholarship, and the Russian histo-
     rian Nikolay Polevoy dedicated his *History of the Russian People* (1830)
     to him. Pushkin was angered by Polevoy's attack on Nikolay Karamzin's
     History of the Russian State (1816–26); he saw this attack as symptomatic
     of a lack of Russian self-respect. In 1826, the year of Karamzin's death,
     Pushkin dedicated to him his one full-length play, *Boris Godunov.* See
     Bethea, "Pushkin as Historical Thinker," in *The Pushkin Handbook*
     (The University of Wisconsin Press, 2005), p. 270.

4   Napoleon's Grande Armée included battalions from twelve countries.

5   A lightweight carriage, often with a hood, for a single passenger.

6   This play by the German playwright August von Kotzebue (1761–1819)
     was popular throughout Europe. Von Kotzebue was fiercely reaction-
     ary; at one time he was an agent in the service of Tsar Alexander I. Bel-
     kin, the novel's supposed narrator/author, gets the name of the heroine
     wrong; it is, in fact, Eulalia.

7   Mostly devoted to theatrical interviews, *The Well-Intentioned* appeared
     irregularly between 1818 and 1826.

8   In his drafts, Pushkin gives this figure his full name. Faddey Bulgarin
     was a writer and journalist who repeatedly attacked not only Pushkin,
     but almost every good writer of his time. After the suppression of the
     Decembrist Revolt in 1825, Bulgarin became an agent in the tsarist se-
     cret police. This passage is dense with allusions to him. Many of the ar-
     ticles published by Bulgarin were taken from the *Hamburg Gazette*, and
     several of his own articles appeared in the *Champion of Enlightenment*
     (1818–25). In 1824, Bulgarin had written "A Promenade along the
     Nevsky." A pea-green coat would have been understood as code for a
     police inspector—even without the subsequent mention of the Police
     Bridge.

9   Prince Rurik (ca. 830–79) was the semilegendary founder of the house
     of Rurikids, from Novgorod. Until 1598, the rulers of Kiev, Vladimir,
     and—later—Muscovy all belonged to this dynasty. Belkin's choice of
     Rurik is an indication of his old-fashioned views.

10   A popular poem, set in a brothel, written by Pushkin's uncle Vasily
     L'vovich Pushkin (1766–1830).

11   Two anonymous satirical poems that circulated in manuscript in the
     early nineteenth century.

12   There is an element of self-parody here. In 1825, while Belkin was supposedly at work, Pushkin was composing his own tragedy, *Boris Godunov*—also about a Russian ruler.

13   Another moment when Belkin's thoughts parody Pushkin's.

14   This too could be said of Pushkin, though more seriously and less parodically.

15   Claude-François-Xavier Millot (1726–85) was a French churchman and historian. His *Histoire universelle* was translated into Russian in 1785.

16   Vasily Tatishchev (1686–1750) was a statesman and ethnographer. His *History of Russia from the Earliest Times* was published posthumously (1768–74). The reliability of his sources was disputed and by 1825 his work was considered obsolete, as was that of his followers Ivan Boltin and Ivan Golikov. Belkin significantly fails to mention Nikolay Karamzin's far greater work.

17   See note 13. Pushkin is thought to have preached to the Boldino peasants that God had sent cholera on them because they had not been paying their quitrent. And in a letter of 29 September 1830, Pushkin wrote to his friend Pletnyov, "I wanted to send you a copy of my sermon to the local peasants. You would have died of laughter" (Paul Debreczeny, *The Other Pushkin*, p. 77).

18   Pushkin himself was then working on *Peter the Great's African*.

19   Edward Gibbon (1737–94) did indeed say something similar on completing his six-volume *The History of the Decline and Fall of the Roman Empire* (1776–88).

20   Another instance of Pushkin making fun of himself. He greatly valued clarity and concision, but Andrey Stepanovich Belkin carries these virtues to an absurd extreme.

21   Since 1803, landowners had had the right, "under certain conditions," to free their serfs.

22   See note 3. Here, the reference to Niebuhr is particularly absurd. Pushkin is parodying the excessive reverence shown him by Polevoy, who had called him "the greatest historian of the age."

23   One of the occasions when Pushkin, since he is writing of the village's golden age, refers to it as Gorokhino. See the afterword, p. 166.

24   Possibly an oblique allusion to a local legend about a young woman supposedly killed by conspirators for passing on information about a plot to murder Ivan the Terrible as he passed through the area during a military

campaign. The tsar ordered a church to be built by the spot where she was buried. See N. K. Gei, *Pushkin—prozaik (Pushkin as a Prose Writer)* (IMLI RAN, 2008), p. 206.

25 An important historical controversy of the time was over whether the origins of Russian culture lie in the Slav world or in Scandinavia. Belkin appears to be arguing for the former, but his earlier remark about the Goriukhinites crossing the Sivka "like the ancient Scandinavians" undermines his case. See Bethea and Davydov, "The [Hi]story of the Village Gorjuxino," p. 302.

26 Catherine the Great held a Grand Legislative Assembly in 1767. The Pugachov Rebellion—the most serious rebellion during the 300 years of the Romanov dynasty—was in part provoked by the stifling of this assembly. This rebellion was clearly one of the "events of note" in which Terenty took part. Pugachov's forces reached the outskirts of Boldino (Gei, *Pushkin*, p. 380).

27 The two-headed eagle, with one head looking west and the other looking east, was a symbol of the Russian state. The state had a monopoly on the sale of alcohol, and an image of the eagle had to be placed at the entrance to every tavern.

28 Alexander Sumarokov (1717–77) was a poet and dramatist, an imitator of French classicism. His rural idylls were remote from the reality of Russian life.

29 The concealment of real names is, of course, inappropriate in what purports to be a work of history. See section two of the afterword, p. 168

DUBROVSKY

1 In a note for *Dubrovsky*, Pushkin wrote, "The splendid year 1762 separated them for a long time. Troyekurov, a relative of Princess Dashkova's, climbed high." It was in 1762 that Catherine (then the empress consort) deposed her husband Peter III and became empress in her own right. Troyekurov evidently took the side of Catherine the Great and her ally Princess Dashkova, whereas Andrey Dubrovsky remained loyal to Peter III and so had to retire from the Guards and live in relative poverty. In this, Dubrovsky resembles both the fictional Andrey Grinyov (the father of the hero of *The Captain's Daughter*) and the real Lev Pushkin (the poet's grandfather); they too paid for their loyalty to Peter III.

2   This formula almost certainly indicates Dubrovsky's readiness to duel. See Irina Reyfman, "Prose Fiction" in Andrew Kahn, ed., *The Cambridge Companion to Pushkin* (Cambridge University Press, 2006), p. 100.

3   Pushkin clearly identifies, at least to some degree, with Dubrovsky. The village near Boldino that Pushkin's father bequeathed to him in 1830 was named Kisteniovo.

4   These details indicate that Troyekurov's father was of humble station. A provincial secretary was at the bottom of the state service hierarchy (thirteenth class), and the rank of collegiate assessor was only eighth class.

5   The dried beetle *Lytta vesicatoria*, or Spanish fly, was used to stimulate the circulation.

6   Pushkin has just told us that Dubrovsky is in, not the Horse Guards, but the Foot Guards. *Dubrovsky* is unfinished; there are other minor inconsistencies. It is possible, though, that Pushkin may have intended the mistake to be seen as Yegorovna's.

7   She means what Russians call "Spring Nicholas's Day," 9 May, the day of the Translation of the Relics of Saint Nicholas from Myra to Bari. St. Nicholas's day itself is 6 December.

8   From Derzhavin's "On the Death of Prince Meshchersky." See p. 184, note 9.

9   The first line of another poem by Derzhavin, celebrating the capture of Izmail from the Turks in 1791. It was set to music by Osip Kozlovsky (1757–1831).

10 A low four-wheeled open carriage.

11 Meeting a priest coming towards you was thought to bring bad luck.

12 Psalm 37:27.

13 The Russo-Turkish war of 1787–91.

14 Johann Lavater, a Swiss poet and philosopher (1741–1801), wrote a long work on the art of judging character from a person's facial features and general build.

15 Yakov Kulnev (1763–1812), an important and popular Russian general from the time of the Napoleonic Wars.

16 Ann Radcliffe (1764–1823), one of the most famous English "Gothic" novelists, was very popular in Russia.

17 Misha, the diminutive of Mikhail, was the name traditionally given to bears.

18 "What does monsieur want?"

19   Schoolboy French for "I want to sleep in your room."

20   "Gladly, monsieur. Please make the necessary arrangements."

21   It was standard practice to fit a second, outer window and frame at the beginning of winter.

22   What he inadvertently says is "Why are you touching? Why are you touching?" What he wishes to say is "Why are you extinguishing? Why are you extinguishing (the candle)?"

23   "Sleep."

24   More schoolboy French, for "I want to talk to you."

25   "What is it, monsieur, what is it?"

26   "Frankly, officer."

27   A Robin Hood figure, the hero of Christian August Vulpius's *Rinaldo Rinaldini* (1797).

28   A legendary rich and generous host.

29   "All these expenses."

30   A reference to the narrative poem "Konrad Wallenrod" (1828), by the great Polish poet, and friend of Pushkin's, Adam Mickiewicz (1798–1855). Musing on the absence of her beloved Konrad, the heroine embroiders a rose in green, and its leaves in red.

31   Or more precisely: the family friend who, in accordance with Russian custom, is substituting for Maria Kirilovna's long-deceased mother.

32   Oak-grove. The hero's surname is derived from this word.

THE EGYPTIAN NIGHTS

1   "Who is that man?" "Oh, he's someone very talented. He can make his voice do anything." "He'd do well, madam, to make himself a pair of trousers with it."

2   "Sir... please excuse me if..."

3   "I believed... I heard... Your Excellency will forgive me..."

4   No doubt because of the censorship, Pushkin deleted the last part of this sentence, from "soliciting donations."

5   "By the body of Bacchus," an exclamation of surprise or wonder.

6   The Italian singer Angelica Catalani (1780-1849) gave concerts in Petersburg in 1820.

7   An opera by Rossini, written in 1813.

8   The last day of Pompeii. Cleopatra and her lovers. Spring seen from a prison. The triumph of Tasso.

9   "Since the great queen had many of them."

AFTERWORD

1   *The Letters of Alexander Pushkin*, ed. J. Thomas Shaw (Indiana University Press, 1963), vol. III, pp. 779–80.

2   T. J. Binyon, *Pushkin: A Biography* (Harper Collins, 2002), p. 417.

3   Svetlana Evdokimova, *Pushkin's Historical Imagination* (Yale University Press, 1999), p. 233

4   Andrei Sinyavsky, *Strolls with Pushkin*, trans. Catharine Theimer Nepomnyashchy and Slava I. Yastremski (Columbia University Press, 2017), p. 94.

5   From the first chapter of *Peter the Great's African*.

6   Svetlana Evdokimova, *Pushkin's Historical Imagination* (Yale University Press, 1999), p. 152.

7   Nepomnyashchy, "The Telltale Black Baby," *Under the Sky of My Africa*, pp. 151–54.

8   "Introduction", ibid., p. 11.

9   "The Telltale Black Baby", ibid., p. 150–57.

10 Bethea and Davydov, "The [Hi]story of the Village Gorjuxino," p. 304.

11 Ibid., p. 305, note 2.

12 Simon Dixon, "Pushkin and History," quoting from Pushkin's essay "On Popular Drama and on M.P. Pogodin's *Martha, the Governor's Wife*," *The Cambridge Companion to Pushkin*, p. 123.

13 Sergei Davydov, "The Evolution of Pushkin's Political Thought," in David M. Bethea, ed., *The Pushkin Handbook* (University of Wisconsin Press, 2005), p. 289.

14 Paul Debreczeny, *The Other Pushkin*, pp. 76–77.

15 D. S. Mirsky, *A History of Russian Literature*, ed. Francis J. Whitfield (Routledge & Kegan Paul, 1968), p. 118.

16 T. J. Binyon, *Pushkin*, p. 250.

17 William Mills Todd III, *Fiction and Society in the Age of Pushkin* (Harvard University Press, 1986), p. 108.

OTHER NEW YORK REVIEW CLASSICS

For a complete list of titles, visit www.nyrb.com.